AF429290

Unequal Temperament

Cheryl Walsh

American Buffalo Books
Manhattan, KS

American Buffalo Books
www.AmericanBuffaloBooks.org

Copyright © 2023 Cheryl Walsh

The Library of Congress has cataloged
the American Buffalo Books paperback as follows:
Names: Walsh, Cheryl, author
Title: Unequal Temperament: a novel / Cheryl Walsh
Description: Manhattan, KS: American Buffalo Books, 2023
Library of Congress Control Number: 2023944972
ISBN: 9798218263935

Printed in the United States of America
1st printing

This is a work of fiction.
It is the product
of the author's imagination,
and any similarities to real people,
living or dead, or actual events
are entirely coincidental.

Peter Grimes by Benjamin Britten and Montagu Slater
© Copyright 1945 by Boosey & Hawkes Music Publishers Ltd.
Reprinted by Permission of B&H Music Publishing, Inc.

Cover design: Jordan Stegeman
Author photo: Bruce Hart

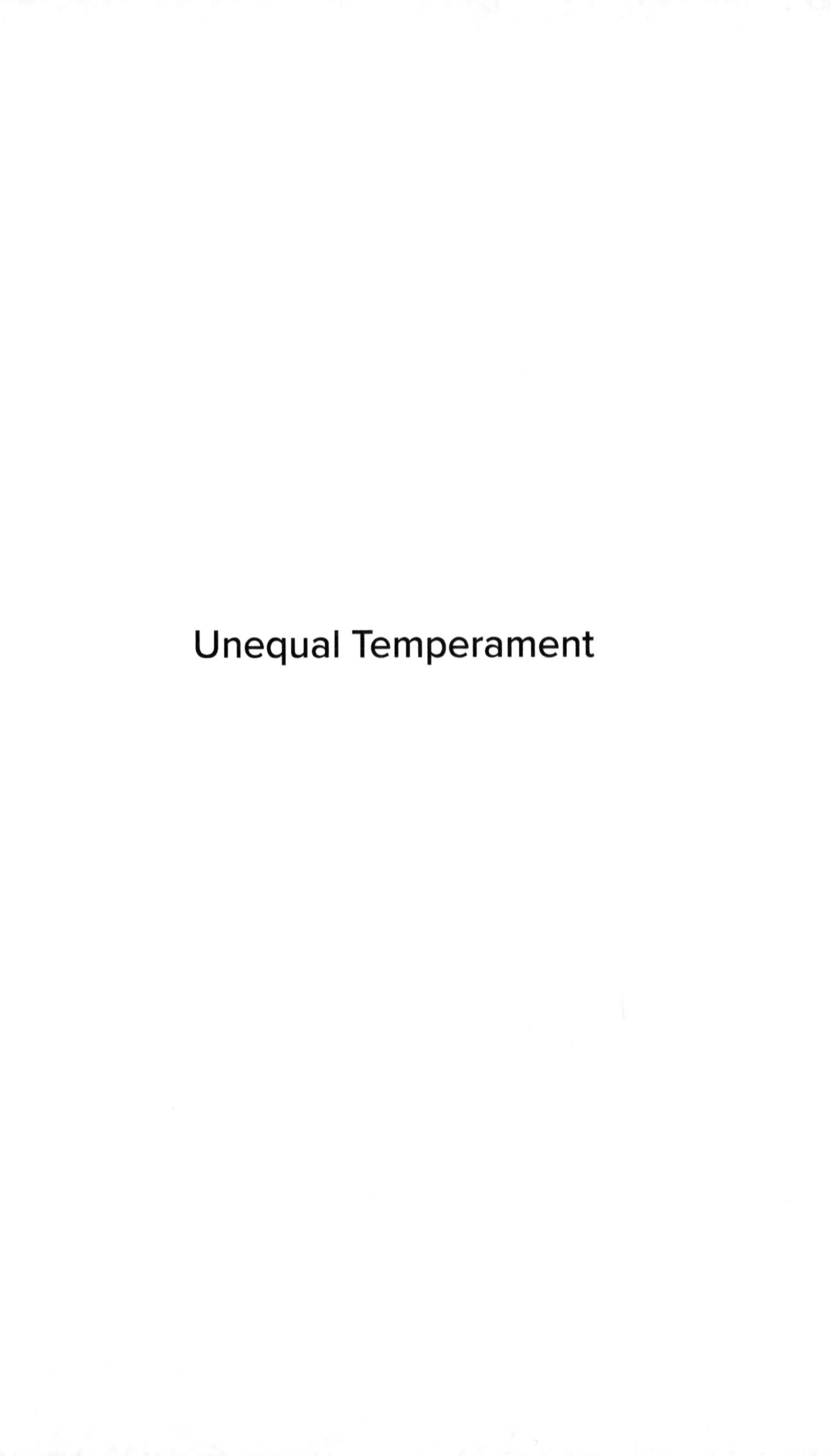

Unequal Temperament

Prelude

Squealing laughter drifted up from the neighbors' yard, where two young children played in the first real snow of the season. It was a distraction even though the window of the music studio was double-glazed and well-insulated. Morgan held her honey-colored hair back from her forehead as if that would help her to listen and sounded an octave on the harpsichord. It was dry but not quite pure—yes, there was a beat, a small pocket of sound like a water droplet condensing on a spider's web. She picked up the tuning hammer, steadied her elbow against the nameboard, and placed the hammer with care on one of the B-flat pins.

For Morgan, tuning a harpsichord was a meditation on the Great Flaw of the musical universe: It was impossible to have all intervals in tune at once. Tune the fifths, and the thirds were too wide. Tune all the thirds, and the fifths were too narrow. Space the twelve tones evenly throughout the octave, as piano tuners did today, and every interval beat with impurity to a greater or lesser extent.

It had been a terrific shock, the revelation of this Great Flaw. When Morgan's first harpsichord teacher explained that equal temperament—the modern standard in tuning—was not "correct" in any absolute sense, it knocked Morgan's entire frame of musical reference irrevocably askew. One half-step was not the same as another? An A-sharp was not necessarily the same as a B-flat?

Morgan squeezed her slender fingers over the head of the tuning hammer and turned it almost imperceptibly until the B-flat octave sounded so dry it was pure desert sunlight uncompromised by humidity. Outside, the children's voices seemed to resonate in the cold air, defying the snow's muffling effect. It irritated Morgan to find herself thinking about the acoustic properties of snow, and she sounded the octave again, just to be sure she hadn't missed any beats. Satisfied, she lifted the hammer gently off the tuning pin, careful not to bend it. Then she sounded the next octave.

As she listened for beats in the tone, her thoughts turned contemplative again. Knowing every chord to be a compromise that violated aural purity had the effect of tempering her customary perfectionism. As Dad so often pointed out, art and purity rarely had much in common. "Purity is just another word for sterility," he'd say. "Imperfection is the real essence of art." And indeed, Morgan had learned to love the Great Flaw, the way it complicated the music, opened up new possibilities. There was beauty in the fact that nothing was ever simple.

Equal half-steps might allow infinite modulations from key to key, but introducing slight inequalities in the distance between tones had its own charms. An unequal temperament rearranged the imperfections that sprang from the Great Flaw so that some intervals could ring pure, while others vibrated with greater dissonance, creating expressive tensions and exquisite spaces in the music. Instead of making all keys sound the same, an unequal temperament endowed each key with its own idiosyncratic delights. Half-steps were not created equal, and pretending they were was not a solution to the Great Flaw. It was merely one way to contend with it. Not a very interesting way either.

Over the years, Morgan had become a connoisseur of unequal temperaments. At the present moment, she was tuning her Kirckman replica harpsichord in preparation for Dad's visit at Christmas. Normally she used the Werckmeister III temperament for Bach, but she wanted to try out a modified Kirnberger to play the g minor prelude and fugue from Book I of *The Well-Tempered Clavier*. She had heard that this Kirnberger brought out the merriment in g minor, and that should suit the prelude admirably, which was as full of wintry drama and cheer as a Dickens Christmas.

A few days ago, she and her husband, Rob, had visited Dad for Thanksgiving. After touring his studio to see the paintings he was working on, they gorged themselves on the traditional feast. As the sun set, Dad sat down at the Steinway—the same one she had played for untold hours as a child—and performed the A-flat major prelude from Book I. Then Morgan played the same piece and continued on with the corresponding fugue. That's what they did whenever they got together: played the same Baroque piece, agreed upon ahead of time. When he visited her, she would play her harpsichord, and he played the upright piano across the room. They'd been sampling *The Well-Tempered Clavier* for quite some time now, though Dad usually stuck to the preludes, while Morgan always included the fugues as well.

"Katie! Be careful!" Tracy, the young mother next door, was calling out to her four-year-old. Her voice scraping through the air broke Morgan's concentration once again. Just let the little girl have some fun, she thought. Her neighbor was such a worrier.

By dint of will and long-practiced concentration, Morgan succeeded in filtering out most of the high-pitched babbling from next door as she sounded the next three octaves, making them all so pure and dry that they were acoustically dead. She couldn't decide whether the dead sound of a perfect octave was a paradox. Free of beats—those sonic conjunctions of frequency and wavelength that occurred whenever two pitches were out of tune—perfect octaves lacked personality, depth, beauty, and anything that might identify them as art. It was a scientific sound, a mathematical value stripped of all emotion. Perfect octaves formed an empty grid—or, as Dad would think of it, a blank canvas—on which the physics of sound could paint sympathetic vibrations and overtones from all three choirs of the harpsichord's strings.

The shrill jangling of a metal bell intruded on her meditation. It was the antique rotary phone in the guest bedroom across the hall. Her irritation having reached critical mass, she put her tuning hammer down. She was almost done, but she decided to play for a while and finish up the last few strings later, once the phone had stopped ringing and the kids had stopped squealing.

She trilled the opening G of the prelude with her right hand, slowly at first and gradually picking up speed, independent of the 16th notes setting a steady rhythm in the left hand. She was proud of that independence of the left and right, an independence hard-schooled at the piano when she was still a child. Faster and faster she drove the long trill until it locked in precise rhythm with the left hand, three notes to each

16th in the bass. The phone rang again, a slightly flat A, not entirely discordant with the G trill.

Dad didn't like trills much, but he would love the bass, the insistence in it, the steadiness, the alternating dissonance and consonance. It seemed to Morgan that the bass was pumping moisture into the air, while the trill made dust fly, high up in the troposphere in a flurry of light—an aerosol around which the moisture would condense and crystallize into snow. The trill resolved into a tumble-down pattern of 16th and 32nd notes, and she thought that Dad would see the snow fly against window panes just as she did, swirling and eddying toward the ground, dancing but not landing.

The bass became more liquid under the second trill, melting snow that the trill pulverized once more into vapor and aerosol. The phone rang a third time as she played that measure again, coaxing more liquid out of the overlapping notes, experimenting with a different tempo of the trill, savoring the fluttering resistance in the middle of each key-stroke as the plectra plucked the strings inside the case.

Morgan followed the dancing snow as it tumbled down and blew back up the staff, as if it were riding the complex drafts that ricocheted off the buildings of a narrow Victorian street. A third trill welled up from the bass—a rumbling of thunder, that rare and wonderful winter phenomenon. The snowflakes above linked up and clung together in the moisture-laden air, stickier and fluffier the closer they came to becoming water again. Soon there would be a conversation in the right hand, near turns tossed back and forth: Shall we be rain? Shall we be snow?

Dad would like this part. The motif was similar to Bach's invention number 14, which he loved to play—they used to talk about how it was like a well-rehearsed comedy team trading quips left and right.

When thunder sounded again even lower in the bass, the storm turned sinister, more like ice than snow. Sustained notes overlapped like smooth layers of rain freezing on contact, not dripping away.

How would Dad see this section? He saw lines and shapes where she saw frontal boundaries, cyclones and anticyclones. But this piece was a microscale phenomenon, and she was in the thick of it, not observing it from a satellite's view. She saw the snow dance around her, heard its conversation with the rain. Dad's painting metaphors would be colors. Colors and textures.

As she reworked the fingering of this section, she realized that Rob was standing in the doorway. He liked to listen to her practice. Sometimes he listened to her for 15 or 20 minutes at a time, just standing in the doorway, and when she was finally done with the piece, he would rub her shoulders and kiss her ear.

The snow rallied in the second half of the piece, breaking free of its coating of sustained notes, finding bits of dust and aerosol still flying around from the trills, bits to cling to, to crystallize against in the higher reaches of the troposphere before drifting back down. And yet there still was ice, long sustained notes undergirding the flights of 16th and 32nd notes, and the conversation returned with a variation: Are we snow? Are we ice? A dusting of snow finally swirled to the earth with a completed turn on a B-natural that lingered on in a trill.

Morgan relished that final trill, trying to see what Dad would see. He always said a Picardy third was like a cool green suddenly turning warm by bursting out yellow. But the major chord felt unstable to her, not green, not yellow, but suspended impatiently between colorless water and air. It leaned into the fugue, longed to continue as she released the keys and heard the damper end the tone.

Outdoors, a child shrieked and began to cry.

Morgan reached up to turn the page, but Rob entered the room, saying her name in a ragged whisper.

Surprised that he would interrupt, she turned and looked up as he stepped behind her and laid his hands on her shoulders. His hands trembled in the moment before they gave her a gentle squeeze. His lips trembled too, and his eyes were red.

Morgan put her hands to his. "What's wrong?" Her voice was dry and barely audible, even to her.

"It's your dad."

Morgan leaned back into his stomach and stopped breathing. She wished that child outside would stop crying.

"He had a heart attack." She felt Rob's diaphragm heave in a sob. She barely heard him say, "He's gone."

One

The edge of a troublesome warm front hesitated in the southeastern quadrant of the regional radar as brilliant patches of time-lapse rain, snow, ice—who knew which was which at the end of the shift?—flitted across Morgan's computer screen. "Are we snow? Are we ice?" she said under her breath, then shook her head violently as she heard herself.

"You OK, Morgan?" Jack asked as he paused behind her workstation. He was an intern, a clean-cut kid from southern Indiana, just out of college.

"I'm getting bleary-eyed, that's all," she said, not taking her eyes from the screen. "Does this look like snow to you?"

"Yes, ma'am." Jack leaned in over her shoulder. "Looks like snow to me. Most of it, leastways. That edge, right along the isobar at Hildesong? Could be a mix."

Morgan changed the color scheme on the reflectivity data, and, as was sometimes the case, she could see distinctions better. A narrow line of a bluer hue popped out where Jack had pointed, the remnant of a bright band. "Good call. Something a little different's happening there, anyway."

"Just talked to a state trooper, said it's some freezing drizzle mixed in," Jack said, explaining away his discerning eye and handing her a scrap of paper with the details. "But all snow now a few miles to the south. Coming down wet and heavy, he said."

For most of the day, there had been freezing rain along the edge of the front with cold rain following once the front had passed. When it stalled out earlier in the day, it looked like the ice build-up would become a problem. Morgan issued a winter storm warning around 10 a.m. for three counties in the southeast. A lot of schools subsequently closed, taking the kids home before cars started sliding off the roads. But after a few hours, the jet stream had angled slightly to the east, shaking loose the low pressure system that was driving the front, and now the low was moving north, pulling the warm sector with it. As the front was on the move again, ice didn't have a chance to build up anywhere.

Morgan, the science and operations officer for the Richfield forecast office, was one of the younger SOOs in the National Weather Service. She loved the job—training the interns and forecasters, running simulations, evaluating verification statistics, keeping up with the leading edge of atmospheric science. But sometimes she found herself itching for the immediacy of forecasting, so she didn't mind busy days like today when she was called back to the operations area.

It was exhilarating at first, keeping up with the flood of data, detecting overall patterns on one screen while sifting for significant details on another, analyzing conflicting computer models, calling observers, reading their text messages. Now, however, it had become just plain exhausting, especially considering all the energy Morgan had to expend not listening to that piece of Bach running through her head. She couldn't remember when it crept into the back of her mind. Are we snow? Are we ice? Sometime in the early afternoon, it must have been.

Jack had gone on to the long-range workstation, and Morgan called to him, "Susan here yet? I'm about done in."

"Yeah, we been run ragged," Jack called back. "All the precip and these temps hovering 'round freezing all day."

Morgan wondered what kind of data Terence had him running over there.

"Anyway," Jack drawled on, "just saw Susan come in. Putting her snacks in the fridge as we speak."

"Rough shift?" Susan's voice rang out from the direction of the break room.

Morgan looked up from her monitor and blinked at Susan making her way through the operations area, one hand resting on her six-months pregnant belly. The Bach welled up in Morgan's mind again, a liquid bass and bright fluttering treble. Her fatigued eyes smarted with tears. "I love you, Susan," she said. "Please take over."

Susan grabbed a chair and sat down next to Morgan. "You OK? You look beat."

"Just tired. And I've got some music stuck in my head that I'm thoroughly sick of. How were the roads driving in?" Susan lived in Clayton County, which was now just behind the front.

"Not bad, if you're a careful driver. Definitely some icy spots. But no trees or power lines down."

Morgan nodded. She didn't like issuing warnings that seemed unnecessary in hindsight, but she was also glad there hadn't been any major damage. "We caught a lucky break when the low started moving north. We've let the storm warnings lapse. There's still an advisory for the southeast counties, and that should probably be extended over the rest of the area because the rain's turning to snow. For the overnight, the main question's how much will fall."

"Hey, before I forget—Terence wants to see you before you go."

Great, Morgan thought. Forget about catching her breath before rehearsal.

Terence was the meteorologist-in-charge, everyone's boss. When Morgan had finished briefing Susan, she found him bent over a computer terminal conferring with Jack and another intern about jet stream data. She waited until the conversation wound down before interrupting.

"Much as I hate to bring you all down to the surface, I need to get going, and Susan said you wanted to see me, Terence."

Terence lifted his head in a crisp nod left over from his military career and led the way to his office on the periphery of the building.

Morgan always imagined him in a uniform, though she'd never seen him in one. He was a taciturn man of average height and far better than average posture, with a deadpan face that nevertheless spoke louder than his few dry words.

He sat down behind his desk, and Morgan remained standing. She didn't want the conversation to last a long time. "You need to get to a rehearsal tonight?"

"That's right, sir." She thought Terence smiled slightly whenever she said sir. "An opera out in Wolverton. *Peter Grimes* by Benjamin Britten.

You should get out to see it at the Civic Center in late March. There's more weather in it than the average opera."

Terence nodded once as if taking the suggestion under advisement. That was a joke, but Terence didn't let on that he had caught it. He said, "I'm concerned about having enough meteorologists to cover the shifts over the next few months. Susan's not due for a while, but I think it would be a good idea to start planning more flexibility into the schedule, while at the same time not asking her to work any overtime."

Morgan nodded. More flexibility while restricting a forecaster's overtime meant that the other meteorologists in the office would need to take a forecasting shift every so often. "So you're worried I won't be available because of rehearsals?"

"No. Just giving you a heads-up."

He handed her the planning schedule for the next three months. Morgan was slated for three swing shifts and a midnight. Only two conflicted with rehearsals, but she knew she could be called in for more. It was nothing new.

She shrugged. "Not a problem."

Terence looked at her as if he weren't finished, but he didn't say anything.

"Is that all? Because I really need to get going."

He nodded, though he was still looking at her intently. As she turned around to leave, he said to her back, "Get some sleep. You look like hell."

"Thanks," she said in her brightest voice and didn't break her stride.

* * *

Back when Morgan had been a forecaster, she had always made up the shift schedule. She had to, to get it to mesh with her rehearsal schedules. It wasn't an odious chore though. She found an aesthetic pleasure in accommodating everyone's requests and making the hours come out right, in finding the combinations of forecasters and interns who had the skills to cover the work and, if she was up to the challenge, who worked well together. It was a lot like designing a temperament, where you had to find the right combinations of in-tune and out-of-tune intervals, combinations that allowed you to play the music you wanted and, if you were up to the challenge, to placate the wolf.

The wolf was that leftover interval that bore the brunt of the Great Flaw: the more in tune the other intervals were, the further out of tune the last interval became. Its dissonance was likened to howling. In early tuning systems, the wolf was often the interval G-sharp to E-flat, and it turned out to be far wider than a perfect fifth. Its howling was so discordant, composers simply wouldn't write in the keys that might require its use. The well-tempered systems of the later Baroque distributed the burden more equitably, allowing fewer intervals to be perfectly in tune, so that the last interval might pass for a fifth. But even so, the wolf still lurked among the sharps and flats of the less common keys. Only with equal temperament did musicians consider the wolf finally banished. Morgan, however, knew the wolf still howled faintly everywhere, in every interval. Modern musicians were simply trained not to hear it.

After a fresh tuning, Morgan used to like sounding the wolf on her harpsichord, listening to the glorious cacophony of beats vibrating in the air: the distillation of imperfection that made beauty possible. There was something noble about the unsung wolf singing for herself.

*   *   *

Morgan stood on the gray-green porch of the house she and Rob had owned for six years. The wooden steps and the porch itself had been swept free of snow, and they would be swept again in the morning. Rob's research on the effect of winter weather on road surfaces and construction materials made him conscientious in that area. She fitted the house key into the lock and hesitated. Light from the kitchen at the back of the house bled through to the bay window next to the porch. A few wet snowflakes danced in the leftover light, flying against the paned window. The Bach prelude flooded her mind, and under her leather gloves, her fingers moved against the keys in her hand, straining to remember the feel of the harpsichord keys.

She was too tired to push the music away again. She nearly felt the anticipation the prelude had inspired weeks ago, as if Dad were still alive and they would see each other soon, play for each other again. That was how the world should feel.

On Morgan's last trip home to Dad's, she had stood in his studio in the light from the big windows along the south wall, where translucent blinds had been drawn against the brightness of the winter sun reflecting off the snow. Her heart stumbled as she took in the canvases in progress that leaned against the east wall. What did people do with an artist's unfinished work? She felt her face twist in pain, and she turned away.

The place smelled of linseed oil and, farther away, as if tucked back in a corner, the clean smell of Fels-Naptha, which he had used to wash his hands. His paints were stored in a large wooden box, open on a battered stand next to an easel in the center of the room. She approached the nearly blank canvas. It was like a baby that was quiet and fed and anticipating her bath. Morgan rubbed her tear-laden eyelashes and shook her head, wondering why that image had come to her. What did she know about babies? What would she ever know?

The canvas had a thin, transparent layer of peachy pink in a lopsided hexagon that took up the lower left-hand third of the area. Dad seemed to have mixed the paints on the canvas, as there were thin streaks of burnt umber and tiny areas of pure vermillion. She wondered if Dad had known where this painting was leading or if he had simply been playing with color. There was no way of knowing, and a sob broke through her knotted throat.

She turned to the paints as if they could give her some kind of answer. The tubes, all partially used, waited in their rightful slots in the open box. A joyfully smeared palette rested in the top of the box, waiting. His small brushes, bristles fresh and clean, stood in a jar next to the box; they were also waiting. Begging to be played with. Two larger brushes lay nearby. They seemed asleep—they'd stopped waiting, and this made Morgan cry even harder.

She hadn't known at the time, but Dad had left all his paints, brushes, and supplies to Rob. Specifically to Rob. Rob liked to draw, and Dad had pressed him to work with pastels a few years ago but hadn't yet convinced him to make the leap to painting. Morgan had never been sure whether Dad's enthusiastic encouragement was wishful thinking or true admiration for Rob's talent. She suspected it was a bit of both because she engaged in both herself. She admired the subtlety of Rob's work, which at times she found both stirring and eerie—so very different in effect from most of Dad's paintings, which were always bold, sometimes playful, and sometimes devastating.

Before Dad's death, she had liked to believe that Rob's work might someday be devastating in its subtlety. Now she couldn't bear the thought of devastating art, and in her grief the last thing she wanted was to feel stirred.

Rob kept Dad's paint box open in the living room. Morgan sometimes ran her fingers over it, touched the paint tubes Dad had touched, and tried to feel close to him, tried to believe the paint in the tube would someday become a miraculous amalgam of tone and shape and texture and rhythm. It was potential. The future. A lie she indulged in.

She had seen Rob indulging in the same lie, running his finger over the scarred surface of the wooden box, over the tubes of paint. Last night, as she was running through some of *Peter Grimes* on the Steinway—Dad's Steinway, now in the alcove at the back of the living room—she had seen him close the box and lift it up, testing its weight. It bothered her, and she stumbled a moment in her playing. Rob looked over his shoulder at her and smiled. Smiled! "So many colors, so little time," he said. Then he left the room.

Morgan had wanted to hide the box, wanted to protect it.

Now she realized it wasn't the prelude running through her mind that kept her from going inside. She didn't want to talk to Rob. He'd want to hear how her day went. He'd tell her if any galleries had called, any collectors. He'd lament that he hadn't heard anything yet about his research grant renewal. Or maybe he'd heard something—the possibility cheered her. Talking about Rob's research was almost soothing in its distance from Dad.

She didn't have time to while away on the porch, and her nose began to sting from the cold. She pushed the door in and was welcomed by the blank wall of the front hall. *Weather Map*, a gift from Dad, had hung there until they had returned home from the funeral. Rob didn't understand why they'd had to take it down, but it was too painful for Morgan to see it every time she walked into the house. Its absence was as much a reminder as its presence would have been, but it seemed to make more sense.

The warm smell of coffee filled the house. Morgan frowned at this and pursed her lips as she hung up her coat. Rob was cheating on his ulcer prevention diet again. He'd started having terrible heartburn several weeks ago and was warned to limit his coffee intake, just when they both needed the comfort of simple daily rituals like sharing a pot of coffee. It was an annoyance to them both, but Morgan saw the necessity.

Rob was sitting at the kitchen table, cradling a ceramic coffee mug Dad had bought for him years ago at an art fair. It was glazed with dark colors and had smooth ridges that fit his hands well.

He looked up from his coffee and greeted her with a guilty half-smile. The light over the table emphasized the fine lines in his face, the beginnings of furrows in his forehead. His curly hair was disheveled but not unusually so. He was glad to see her, as if he had been waiting a long time for her to show up. Morgan sensed he was upset about something, wanted to talk, but she was afraid to ask what was wrong. She knew, however, she couldn't very well get out of it.

"So what's with the coffee?"

"It's decaf." His voice was flat. He lost the half-smile and looked down at the table.

"Still rots your stomach." Morgan didn't like the shrewish note she heard in her voice, but she didn't know how to apologize for it. She put her purse on the table and stepped over to the coffee maker. She poured the last half-cup of coffee into a mug pulled from a hook above the counter.

"It stains your teeth too," Rob said, looking up at her again. She lifted her mug in an imitation of a toast and took a sip. Rob smiled and did likewise. She was glad he smiled.

The coffee had been sitting on the burner a while and was pretty strong. Bitter. There was some chicken noodle soup from a can warming on the stove, but she didn't feel hungry.

She stood by the counter and waited for Rob to say something. When he shifted in his seat, she said, "If you don't want to tell me what's wrong, that's just fine with me. Because, frankly, I've had a rough day."

Rob turned back. "Why?" he asked, looking alarmed.

She sat down opposite him at the table. "You first."

He shook his head with urgency. "Tell me what happened."

"Oh for crying out loud—nothing so bad. Just a long day of indecisive precip—you know—is it going to be rain, is it going to be ice? I issued a warning that turned out not all that necessary. Which is good—that it wasn't needed. I just wish I'd seen that the system would be traveling north."

"It got pretty icy in Wolverton. I was glad for the warning."

She tried to smile but ended up saying, "You're too generous."

"I saw your name on the warning when I checked the forecast at lunchtime. Could tell they'd pulled you into forecasting."

Morgan caught sight of a teething ring underneath the table and picked it up. It was a little slimy, and she grimaced. "What is this?"

"It's a teething ring."

"I can see that. Where'd it come from?"

"Tracy came over a little while ago and brought the kids along. Guess little Mac dropped it."

She dropped the ring back on the floor, not wanting to put it on the table.

"Stu's in Fort Wayne on business," he went on, "and he couldn't make it home for some reason. Maybe the weather? Poor kid's stir-crazy—dying to talk to an adult for a few minutes. So I made some coffee."

"See what I mean? Generous to a fault."

He sighed, as if concurring with her assessment of his character flaws, and looked off into the open emptiness of the dining room. There was definitely something wrong.

"So did you tell *her* what's bothering you?"

"Didn't get a chance." He paused and looked into his coffee before taking a quick gulp. "Besides, I wanted to talk to you."

"Then talk to me. I have to leave for rehearsal soon, and I really should get something to eat."

She started to get up, but Rob touched her hand, and she realized she had to stay. She settled back into the chair, looking at him. Disappointment, failure, was written all over his face.

"So what's wrong? You've got me worried now, so spit it out." She wanted to apologize, but for God's sake, the guy drove her crazy sometimes. She made a conscious effort to be gentle with her next utterance: "Out with it."

"OK." He took a deep breath. "NSF isn't renewing my grant."

A cold wind blew through her chest and out her mouth. "That's . . . disappointing." Unexpected.

"Yeah," he said. "Yeah. So much for the fast track to full professor. All this talk of cutbacks, and they actually expanded funding for road research this year. But they didn't renew my grant—gave more money instead for a couple of new projects—in the South for Christ's sake! It was a competitive renewal, and I guess I just couldn't compete."

"Don't feel sorry for yourself." She took a big gulp of bitter coffee. "I can't stand that." That didn't come out right—she hated the way it sounded. What she meant—it wasn't selfishness. He was moving too fast. This news was moving too fast.

"Is that all you have to say?" He looked at her, his light brown eyes hurt and uncomprehending. Then he gave up and looked down.

Not that look. She couldn't take that defeated look, that bury-your-head-in-the-coffee-mug down-and-out look. "I'm sorry." She felt herself start to cry and focused on swallowing it. "What more can I say? I don't have the money for your research. I wish I did."

A long time ago, she was sure of it, she had known the words to say. But she had lost them. She put her head in her hands, and it felt good to have it supported by something other than her neck.

"Life goes on," she tried again. "We can't feel sorry for ourselves. Life goes on." Her tears spilled onto the table. She took a deep breath, clenched her jaw, and willed the tears out of her eyes. "Everyone has successes and disappointments. You get a gig, you lose a gig." She sat up just as Rob reached out to touch her. "You'll survive."

Of course he'll survive, she thought. His heart is fine. It's generous and fine.

Oh God. She had to do something.

She got up from the table and strode through the dining room, through the front hall and into the living room, back to the Steinway. Dad's Steinway. She didn't know what to play, and she didn't have time to search through music. "Everyone loses gigs," she muttered to herself. Her hands played a few bars from the opening of Act II of *Peter Grimes*. A hymn of all things, sung by the hypocritical townsfolk. She broke off and sat in silence for five seconds. Then she attacked Chopin's "Butterfly" etude. She hated Chopin. But it proved to her she could do what she hated.

*   *   *

Eighteen years before, in her last year of high school, Morgan had been the last audition of the day at the Mount Hope Conservatory of Music.

Universally praised by her teachers since she could remember, she had been unprepared for Leo Neville's sneering whine after her last audition piece: "You don't have the hands for Chopin!"

Holding his forehead with the tips of his fingers, he said, "Every year, I have to listen to every Hélène Grimaud wannabe in the Midwest mangle Beethoven and Chopin. Really, Miss Tallis, spare me." The two other professors on the panel objected to his comments, but Neville wasn't about to rein himself in. He walked over to her, picked up her cold right hand and pulled the fingers apart. He said, "You want to be a concert pianist? You can't even reach an octave between your second and fifth fingers." He shook his head with impatience. "Do yourself a favor. Don't torture yourself or your audience. You don't have a chance."

Morgan was stunned. Even if she had played badly she wouldn't have expected such insults. And she hadn't played badly! The Bach fugue was flawless, the Beethoven was precise but impassioned, and the Chopin—it was true it was her weakest piece, but technically, she had played it perfectly. The tempo was a tad irregular, but it wasn't like she had stumbled through it—and what's the matter with a little rubato? It was romantic for God's sake! Short of brilliant maybe but far more than competent. Just where did that bastard get off telling her she didn't have what it takes?

Her offended hand flushed with anger as Neville dropped it into her lap, and she hardened her mouth into a stiff line. The rest of the panel thanked her, assured her that she'd had an excellent audition, with profuse apologies for the rudeness of their colleague. "He always gets like this toward the end of audition week," one of the professors offered. "And it has been a very long day."

"The length of the day doesn't change the incompetence of the pianist," Neville tossed back.

Morgan didn't remember leaving the audition room. She remembered only how she had stood on the marble steps outside the recital hall, watching a west Michigan sunset redden the fog rising off a four-inch snow pack. She didn't think—it was more elemental than that. She simply knew she would do whatever it took to prove Leo Neville wrong.

*   *   *

She thought of Leo Neville now, that arrogant fool who just happened to have been right. It made her angry. But that was the point of playing the "Butterfly" etude. It was an exercise in channeling anger into delicacy. She hit the notes with a confidence borne of an intimate knowledge that people rarely have of their nemeses. She could not play the piece with love, but she did play it with passion. This butterfly did not flit benignly from buttercup to buttercup. Rather, it exercised a delicate form of torture, as if tickling the flowers to death.

She played it perfectly even though her hands were tired and she sometimes felt a twinge in her left wrist, where she had injured a tendon long ago. She moved into the last few bars, pedal down for almost four measures while her right hand fluttered repeatedly over the same 16th notes and her left hand hopped with delicacy up and then down the keys. Then the pedal came up, and she finished with staccato octaves in the left and a final pianissimo flutter in the right.

There was a singular satisfaction in a flawless performance of this piece, the same that a schoolyard bully might feel in worming his way out of punishment. At least she didn't feel sorry for herself.

She felt a kind of movement, an eddying in an air current. She turned and saw Rob, leaning against the entrance to the alcove, taking a sip of coffee. His eyes looked puffy, like they did when he wanted to cry and forced himself not to. All of a sudden she was aware of all the flecks of gray in his brown hair. She felt the hard edges of her face melt, but she couldn't reach out to him, even though she wanted to, knew he wanted her to. Maybe if there weren't that damned coffee mug between them. Why couldn't anything ever be simple?

"We'll be all right, Morgan." He looked as if he might be asking a question.

She looked down at the keys of the piano and felt her nose stinging. "I have to get to rehearsal."

Rob

Lately, Morgan is all points and hard edges. She's, I don't know, break-able, like a crystal with no fracture resistance. You just know it's going to snap any minute under its own weight. No plasticity. I wish she would do something to soften her suffering—tune her harpsichord, play Bach inventions ... something. I mean, I loved him, too, but he wouldn't want us to bury ourselves in grief. She has to know that.

It's almost like Morgan's grief is some kind of control system that is suddenly operating on our marriage, regulating the temperature and pH to keep her stuck in preset reactions. But I can't tell if the environment is more acidic or more basic, what effect heating or chilling would have—so what do I do to disrupt the control loops? And maybe chemistry is totally the wrong analogy anyway. Maybe the grief is simply a load that's too heavy for the superstructure of our relationship. In that case, all I can do is try to be that much more supportive, shore up any beam that's approaching a bending moment. In the meantime, I think I'm approaching my own compression limit.

This is all hard work. And no play—that's what's missing. Morgan doesn't play anymore. When she took this opera gig at Heritage Midwest, I thought it was a good idea, hoped it would set her in a new direction where we could meet up again on the other side of this grief. But it's just more work. She does it willingly, throws herself into it, but she's not having fun. She's not *playing*. Since Dad died, she hasn't touched her harpsichord.

I miss her playfulness. It's what I always looked forward to when I came home at night.

Her playfulness is what caught my attention when I first met her. She winked at me. In acoustics, the only class we ever took together. It was after I'd asked some confused question about sound waves. I've forgotten the question; I remember the wink. I probably turned red. Then she was waiting for me after class—she gave me a flyer from her backpack—an ad for an Early Music Society concert. "Come see sound waves in action," she said. Then she gave me the look.

It's almost mocking, the look. She raises her eyebrows a little, narrows her eyes ever so slightly, and looks at me sidelong. One corner of her mouth smiles like she's telling me a joke that only I will understand. At that instant, it gave me the feeling that we were inside an intimate moment, just the two of us. Then she smiled, close-lipped, and walked away without saying anything else. Halfway down the hall, she looked over her shoulder to see me still standing there. She laughed and shot me a beautiful grin, and the force of it hit me like a shock wave.

So of course I went to her concert. The first half bored me silly. I didn't know anything about Baroque music in the first place, so what was I supposed to make of all those crumhorns, sackbuts, and viola da gambas. I couldn't tell you what was played, but it was slow and heavy, like a steamroller moving at a snail's pace. I mean, there had to be structure to it, but I didn't know enough at the time to identify it.

At intermission, Morgan tuned the harpsichord, which struck me as kind of funny. I mean, it looked like a piano, only with two keyboards, and I'd never seen anyone tune a piano in the middle of a concert. So I spent the second half trying to hear some change in the harpsichord, but I didn't know enough to know what to listen for. The music was a lot jollier though. Morgan's hands were busy—intricate finger play all over both keyboards. The conductor had her take a solo bow at the end of the piece. I wanted to cheer, but I was afraid of violating some protocol.

I hung around after the concert and watched her receive compliments in the auditorium lobby from the many bluehairs in the audience. She wore a sleeveless black gown. I thought she looked happy enough, like she'd done well, but when she saw me, her face lit up as if she wanted every one of her small white teeth to flash in my eyes. I was dazzled. Tongue-tied too. I could feel my face getting warm. "You were great," I managed to say. Somehow in my halting conversation I ended up asking her why the harpsichord needed to be tuned at intermission.

She said that she wasn't adjusting the temperament or anything, just tuning a few notes that seemed to be ringing false. When I asked her what a temperament was, she pulled me back into the auditorium by my arm. "You'll love this!" she said.

She explained how a single vibrating string produces sound waves at a fundamental frequency, as well as a whole series of subsidiary frequencies called overtones. That wasn't news to me, since you learn that in acoustics, so it was pretty easy to follow what she was saying. What I didn't know, or had never thought about, was that so much in music was defined in terms of the relationship between the frequencies of pitches.

"When musicians say an interval is 'out of tune,'" Morgan was saying, "they mean that two pitches' frequencies are out of sync. Or out of sync to an unacceptable extent because these days all intervals except octaves are out of sync and musicians are trained to hear them that way and like it." She looked down at the harpsichord. "If Baroque composers heard their music played on a piano, they'd think it was really out of tune. Especially thirds—they're way off." Her hand dropped down to the upper keyboard and played what I guess was a third. "And a modern musician thinks thirds on a harpsichord sound funny. It's all a matter of what you're used to."

"So why'd musicians get used to hearing out-of-tune intervals?"

"It's the Great Flaw." She sighed, not like she was sad, but like she was relishing something. "You can't have all intervals in tune at once." She turned to me and shook her head with mock sadness. Then she turned back to the harpsichord. "Take those out-of-tune thirds. Three major thirds make an octave." She played a series of notes. "The frequency ratio of a pure major third is five to four. Multiply that three times and you get 125 to 64."

"And that's a problem?"

"An octave has to be two to one."

"So you're what? Three 64ths short?"

"Exactly." She squeezed my arm. "You can really hear the difference. And if there's one thing everyone agrees on, it's that octaves have to be in tune. So you could have a tuning system—a temperament—where two of these thirds are in tune, and the other will be way off to make the octave pure. If you have to use that last third, it'll howl." She gave me a mischievous look, and the pleasant shock wave left me breathless for a second. "The biggest howler is called the wolf. In the nineteenth century, more and more musicians opted to have everything a little out of tune in order to avoid having a wolf."

"But not harpsichordists."

"No, we love the wolf." She flashed me a brilliant smile, and I lost my breath again. "We need to have at least some intervals pure, or nearly pure, in order for the instrument to sound right." She lifted the lid of the harpsichord higher so I could look inside the case. "A harpsichord has lots of strings—usually three sets, or choirs." I found it hard to tear my eyes away from her, but I saw, as she promised, lots of delicate-looking strings. "The sound relies on sympathetic vibrations—sound waves resonating in strings that haven't been plucked. That's the key to understanding the harpsichord. If too many intervals aren't at least close to pure, when one string sounds, there's no resonance in any of the other strings. There's no brilliance, it's just dull. Dead sound that doesn't go anywhere."

That sounds like our life right now. Functional but with no connections or resonance. Like an afocal system where the light beam never converges. Nothing is illuminated, but the light doesn't disperse. We're just going along on our parallel paths without meeting.

When I got the word that my grant proposal was rejected, all I wanted was to hear Morgan tell me it would be OK. To say she had confidence in me. To give me a hug or even a smile. Let me know we were still connected, able to bear the load of disappointment together. Something. And she couldn't do that. Couldn't do one simple thing that would've made me feel better.

At first, I thought she just didn't care. But then she was trying so hard to keep everything in that she was shaking. And all I could do was sit there and watch—I couldn't even touch her. I was so afraid she would fall apart. Because I don't know what's wrong, I'm so afraid of making it worse.

When she got up, I hoped she was going upstairs to the harpsichord. I hoped she would break down, cry all over the keys, then maybe we could find our way from there to repair what's broken between us. But, no, she went to the piano, started playing that damned Chopin. I wanted to cry. She sneers when she plays that piece, a sneer full of sharp teeth. There's no room for me when she has that look on her face.

Sometimes I dream of being penned up with a wolf, a snarling wolf. I don't know if there's a way out because I have to focus on the wolf. I can't investigate the pen's structure, how it's designed or how strong it is. The wolf is in a corner, afraid to attack me, but ready if I threaten it. It's not like I want to hurt it—I want to be friends. But if I reach out, something bad will happen.

I feel like Morgan has chosen her corner. And tonight I'm afraid to go to sleep.

She sometimes used to talk about herself as the wolf. Taking on the thankless role of accompanist, someone who does all the grunt work so that others can claim the glory. That was fine with her. It's a noble calling, she'd say, taking the back seat. "It's where the real action is anyway." Then she'd give me the look.

I used to wake up some nights and hear her playing, faintly, long after midnight. It was too soft to really wake me, but still, it was designed to wake me. Always some kind of seductive dance. I'd make my way up to her studio in a sleepy daze, led on by the rhythm—it always called to mind some bold image of power or audacity, like a skyscraper or a satellite. It was strident. Structural. But sensuous. Those late-night pieces were never Baroque because they were for *me*—she played what she knew I'd like, what she knew would draw me out.

One time—no, many times—I stood in the doorway to her studio, watching, listening. She knew exactly what she was doing. She was bluish white in the moonlight, wearing something filmy that left her shoulders bare. Delicate beads of sweat on her shoulders, her forehead, her lip. Her head bent over the two keyboards, pulsing like the music, nodding to the left or right, eyes widening here, narrowing there. When she finished, she held the last chord, hands still on the keys, until every sound faded out. It took forever too, as if our desire created infrasound or some kind of radiant power that kept the strings vibrating.

Finally, she looked up at me. Slightly crooked smile. Supremely confident. Suddenly I was around her, hand in her hair, an arm cradling the small of her back, lips on her lips, then on her ear, and she shivered, let out a breathy cry. I felt her pulse on my tongue, tasted the salt on her breast.

We made love on a smooth white sheet she had spread out on the carpet. She kissed me, everywhere at once, whispered so many things in my ear and I missed them all—they were drowned out by the rushing of blood through my veins.

I want those words back. I asked her what they were, told her I wanted to know. She sat up and laughed. Like she was happy. Then she gave me the look and bayed at the moon.

Two

Peter Grimes, one of the most popular 20th-century operas, takes place in a small village on the English coast in the early 1800s. Peter, a local fisherman on the margins of society, becomes a complete pariah when his young apprentice dies at sea. In the opera's prologue, an inquest rules the death accidental, but it does nothing to clear Peter in the townsfolk's eyes. Nevertheless, Peter remains in the village, rooted to the place as much by his desire to gall the gossips as by his attachment to the widowed schoolmistress, Ellen Orford. With her help, he obtains another apprentice from the workhouse. When it becomes clear that Peter is overworking and mistreating the boy, Ellen tries to persuade him to be a good and kind master. But Peter turns on her, blinded by his desire to silence the gossips, who "listen to money, only to money." The townsfolk, some of whom have spied on Ellen's conversation with Peter, march upon Peter's hut to call him to account.

The hut has a precarious perch on a cliff eroded by recent storms. As the townspeople make their way up the hill, the apprentice falls to his death—another accident but hardly an unforeseeable one. Peter scrambles down the cliff in hopes of helping the boy, and the hut is empty when Peter's accusers arrive. A few days later, Ellen finds the apprentice's shirt near the tidemark and suspects the worst. When she and a sympathetic sea captain, Balstrode, catch up to Peter, he is mad with exhaustion, disappointment, guilt, and grief. Balstrode urges him to take his boat out from the shore and scuttle it. And as Peter sails away to his death, a new day dawns in the village.

It was clear that Britten's sympathies lay with the persecuted fisherman, the misfit who, in many ways, was just fulfilling expectations. In reference to *Peter Grimes*, Britten once said, "the more vicious the society, the more vicious the individual."

Morgan, however, didn't buy it. Although she loved much of Britten's music and was excited to be working on one of his operas, she didn't like his hero. She found it hard to forgive his habit of losing his apprentices. Maybe he didn't murder them outright but, well, dead was dead. It was true there wasn't much to like about the townsfolk either, whose concern for the apprentice grew primarily out of malice toward Peter and whose unforgiving hypocrisy contributed to the apprentice's plight. Then there was Ellen Orford, whom Morgan didn't understand at all—why was she attracted to Peter in the first place? And how could that attraction have been so strong that it blinded her to the danger the poor apprentice was in? Morgan didn't have much patience for people whose lives were ruled by wishful thinking. About the only character she did like was Balstrode, and then he ended up telling Peter to commit suicide.

That was another thing that made her uncomfortable: suicide as a practical solution. Vicious society, vicious individuals—yes, certainly, there were plenty of both. But one was not an excuse for the other. Nothing was ever that simple.

Morgan picked her way with care toward the Wolverton Civic Center in the dim light of the city parking lot. She was late. The 25-minute drive from Richfield had taken 40 minutes because snow flurries cut down on visibility and there were patches of ice on the highway. The afternoon's freezing rain was still dangerous on the unsalted parking lot, and the fresh snow wasn't deep enough to provide much traction for Morgan's boots. Looking down was the opposite of her instinct, and it annoyed her. She planted her feet wide for a moment and looked into the dark sky heavy with swirling snow.

She found herself recalling a winter day early in her marriage. She had been in a cold, unfamiliar room where Rob was sitting on a low stool in a hospital gown. He looked up at her with a sloppy embarrassed smile.

"This was a good idea, right?"

She remembered putting her hand to his face and kissing him gently, giving him freely all the reassurance she had. But now she didn't have any reassurance left, and it made her angry to think that he could be so greedy for it right now.

She didn't like how the ice made her stand still, and she started walking again. When she opened the door to the Civic Center, warm air billowed out in accordance with the steep pressure gradient, ruffling the flyers tacked up on the large bulletin board at the end of the lobby. The second orchestral interlude from *Peter Grimes* swelled in her mind, just as it did in the opera's tavern scene whenever anyone came through the door. She smiled. The opera's interludes were terribly evocative of weather, by far the best part of the work. As the rehearsal accompanist, she didn't get to play the interludes themselves, but parts of them spilled over into the scenes and wove their way into the arias, creating atmosphere, recalling the sea.

A raked corridor ran off the theatre lobby, tucked behind the stairs to the balcony. It led down to the other side of the building and below the main stage, where the Heritage Midwest Opera Company rented a large black box area. The first blocking rehearsal for the chorus was this evening, to start in about twenty minutes, and before that, Morgan was supposed to work with Ford Trimble, who was playing Peter Grimes.

She heard Ford playing the studio piano now, the storm music from the tavern scene of all things. She burst through the door just as the music receded.

"Your timing is a little off," Morgan said.

"I'd say it's your timing that's off. '*O tide, that waits for no man, spare our coasts!*' You can't very well expect me to hold off on the music while you choose your moment."

He was right of course, but it was easy to ignore that. "Those lyrics aren't even in that scene."

Ford continued to play without replying and started to sing the part of Balstrode.

"Don't strain your voice," Morgan teased. "You're no baritone."

He gave her an irritated look, but he stopped singing.

Ford was a tenor, a nearly great tenor in fact—and near greatness can be almost a tragedy for an opera singer. He was 48, his dark brown hair on its way to silver, his chiseled face aging very well, square jaw and strong chin compensating for a somewhat too large mouth full of big, straight teeth. He'd had an early career in Europe, though not at anyplace like La Scala or Paris. He'd been making a good living, but for some reason he'd decided to come back to a faculty position at Wolverton State. Homesick perhaps. Morgan had known him close to 10 years, and she had the impression that behind his bravado he was disappointed in himself.

She put a boxed set of CDs atop the piano. Ford was dressed down more than usual, in jeans and a brushed twill shirt. Another day she might have teased him about trying to get into character. Now she just thanked him for lending her his recording of *Peter Grimes*. "I really liked Jon Vickers' take on it. Though I think you'd be better off taking your cue from Peter Pears."

He kept playing. "Who asked you?" he said with a sardonic twist of the mouth.

"You did. Pears is more reserved and—intelligent, I guess. More the lyric tenor. It would suit your voice better. Vickers seems almost reckless—"

"Exactly. Grimes is reckless, passionate. Not intelligent, not reserved."

Morgan shrugged. "Then they cast the wrong voice." She turned away and sat down in one of the folding chairs strewn around the room. She closed her eyes.

Ford's playing trailed off. "It's not like you to insult me and not glory in the reaction."

"I don't care what your reaction is. And only you would take the term intelligent as an insult." She opened her eyes and observed Ford's puzzled expression. "I'm sorry I'm late. I stopped at home after work and took a little too long getting away again."

Morgan thought it was silly to rehearse with Ford anyway. He was an accomplished pianist and could work out his parts for himself. But he liked focusing on his singing rather than playing. And he liked Morgan.

"Well, I hope Rob made the delay worth your while," Ford said. "As for me, I'm sick with disappointment. Maybe we could have a more private session in one of the studios upstairs and you could console me."

"Is it me, or are your propositions becoming more insulting lately?"

"It's you." Ford's left hand fluttered over the keys in a soft bass tremolo. "I'm more in awe of you all the time."

"Sometimes I wonder what you would do if I actually took you up on it."

"It would be simple enough to find out." He smiled at her, and the tremolo went silent.

"No. It wouldn't." She looked at him hard and was surprised to feel offended. "It would be very complicated."

Ford played a few desultory bars of his first aria, *What harbour can embrace terrors and tragedies?* He looked back, and his smile turned sly. He asked, "So how's good old Rob?" He played the next phrase, *With her there'll be no quarrels.*

"Fine." She started rummaging through her portfolio for her score. "Actually, he's not fine. He found out today that he didn't get a grant he'd applied for."

"Oh. I see why you were late. Consolation." He started to plunk out a bawdy melody from Act III.

"Knock it off, Ford."

He caught the edge in her voice and stopped. "A big grant then?"

She nodded.

"What was it for?"

"Building better highways. Research on road surfaces, how they react to weather conditions. You know, what he does. His life's work."

Ford's right hand slipped onto the keys again and back into Act I. *What harbour shelters peace?* "So what happens now?" *Away from tidal waves, away from storms?*

"Nothing terrible." Why couldn't she have said even that much to Rob? "Heavier course load, slower progress on research. He's afraid he won't make full professor, though that's his bruised ego talking more than anything. It'll just take longer." She yawned and tried to sit up straight. "Do you mind if we reschedule? The chorus is going to start showing up any time now anyway."

Ford looked at her. His eyes were serious. Careful. Then he smiled, shook his head, and waved his hand toward the door. "Go on. I think you skipped dinner. I think you're hungry."

Morgan nodded and sighed and dragged herself off in search of food.

*   *   *

Years before, late in her first semester at Mount Hope Conservatory, Morgan had been 19 years old, hungry, cold, and beyond tired. In her third straight week of four-hours-per-night sleep, a mean wind started to blow from the northwest across Lake Michigan, whistling through the cracks of old, drafty Drysdale Hall and dumping heavy lake-effect snow onto the campus. That night, around 10 p.m. Morgan was practicing, and, as usual, her hands were freezing. It got to the point where Chopin's "Butterfly" etude sounded like a rhinoceros with a limp, so Morgan stumbled into the corridor toward the women's room to soak her hands in a sink of hot water.

The random meanderings of a violin and a saxophone floated down the hall from other practice rooms. In her caffeine-jangled state, she heard them as an eerie *danse macabre*. A flute contributed a frightened bird whose invisible wings beat about Morgan's face until she shooed it away. The familiar smells of woodwind reeds and cork grease brought her back to her high school's band room, and she tried to remember whether the bird belonged to the oboe solo or clarinet trio she had to accompany at solo and ensemble festival.

When Morgan reached the restroom, she heard tiny chips of rock candy pelting the window from the darkness outside. That was the work of the bright green monster who glowed like a weather map, just out of sight. "He must be pretty happy with the wind chill," she muttered as she plunged her hands into a steaming sink. Hot pins on the surface of her skin blossomed into gradual warmth. Around her, the bits of scales and scraps of jazz in the air rearranged themselves into a fugue. She fingered a mordent under water on the white enamel of the sink, then she started with a different finger and inverted it. "I wish they'd let me play some Bach," she said.

What she really wanted, though, was to sleep for a few days. But Chopin was waiting down the hall, in league with the weather monster and caffeine, and she doubted she would ever sleep again.

It was such a sad and hopeless thought. Chopin would always be waiting. Her fresh warm hands might be able to heal the rhinoceros's lame foot, but it would never become a butterfly. She heard Leo Neville laugh into her ear, freezing the incipient warmth in her hands with pricks of rock candy sleet. "You don't have the hands for Chopin!"

Most of the time, she could count on the thought of Neville to jump start her ambition, but at that dark, cold moment, it occurred to her that he might have a point after all.

She looked at her slender, frail fingers, seeking reassurance. She stretched them out, trying to make them bigger, and all of a sudden she saw the problem. They were webbed. "No wonder!" she whispered. She fished her keys out of the pocket of her now loose jeans, wet hand scraping against the denim, and opened the small penknife she kept on her key chain. She tried to cut the translucent flesh between her second and third fingers, but nothing happened. The knife passed right through, and the webbing remained intact. She didn't bleed until the knifepoint reached the flesh of her hand between her fingers, but even then, the webbing was unbroken.

Panic swept through Morgan like an Alberta clipper, swift and cold. The webbing would never be gone. She would never play Chopin. She was living proof that Leo Neville was right.

The small drops of blood dissipated in the watery bowl of the sink, and she could barely see the stinging cut as she stared down at her hands. But then another possibility struck her: two red lines carved into her wrist and stretching half-way to the elbow. She could sleep that way maybe.

She didn't remember the knife cutting into her skin, slicing into her tendon, but she did remember how the cold caffeine coursing through her veins gushed out in beautiful swirls of bright red in the white sink. It could have been one of Dad's paintings. Leo Neville was gone, the weather monster sighed and slipped away, and she felt warm and grateful as she sank to the floor, sleepier than she had ever been in her life.

Sleep deprivation, Morgan had told the doctor when she woke up in the Mount Hope infirmary. Honestly, she had no desire to die. She had way too much to do. Another etude and two nocturnes before the end of the semester. Not to mention a Beethoven sonata and that damned Rachmaninoff she could never play straight through without some minor disaster. After a good night's sleep, she was confident she had a handle on desperation. She promised the doctor and social worker she would get at least six hours of sleep per night from then on.

They didn't believe her, and neither did Dad.

* * *

Seventeen years later, Morgan sat on a bench next to a vending machine deep inside the Wolverton Civic Center, chewing peanut butter crackers and leaning against the machine's vibrating hum while she waited for the rehearsal to start. She was on her second package of crackers to relieve the dull ache of hunger she hadn't noticed. That was convenient, she thought, being unaware of hunger. But it disturbed her too. She thought of how long it had been since she had baked an apple pie or made cherry turnovers—Rob's favorite. She used to love having him in the kitchen as she cut the dough, listening to him explain the physics of perfect pastry or the chemistry of sugar and cherries. She didn't know why that seemed so impossible now.

Her size six khakis hung loose on her, and her body seemed to be growing sharp all over. She really had lost the weight everyone kept telling her she had. And she probably did look like hell, as Terence had put it. With a mental shrug she thought, grief does that to people. Then she put those thoughts out of her mind.

But even though she refused to think about it, uneasiness nagged her. Was it really grief? It felt more like a burden than a loss. Like guilt or shame. Or at the very least, unfinished business.

The sounds of singers straggling in floated down the corridor and around the corner into the vending niche. A few of the more dramatic ones chattered in raucous tones interspersed with loud laughter. Others (the sopranos) spoke in a hushed breathy *sotto voce* that could be almost as histrionic, though better for the vocal cords. She heard some people humming low tones and others singing snatches of scales or arpeggios on every imaginable syllable.

Morgan wondered whether to give Charles the bad news about her schedule before rehearsal or after. For most directors, a couple of adjustments wouldn't be much of a problem, but Charles was something of a bratty wunderkind, and he had the reputation of making a big unreasonable deal about everything. They hadn't worked together before, but Morgan already sensed that changes he himself didn't initiate wouldn't be welcome.

She made her way along the corridor, finding herself tensed as if she were still on ice, and indeed the waxed tiles did seem slippery. She stepped into the rehearsal space, which was loud with voices and the sliding of chairs across the floor as Charles directed the set up of rows for the chorus. It was clear he intended to rehearse the music before blocking the scenes, even though Morgan had already rehearsed the chorus several times for this act.

It irritated her, this inefficient lack of trust in her abilities, but then, they hadn't worked together before, so she supposed he had the right to doublecheck her work. Morgan approached him with a tired smile, conventional greeting, and an apology for bringing bad news.

Charles frowned. "What's the bad news?"

"I won't be available for a couple of rehearsals—the fifth and the 19th. We're having some scheduling constraints on my day job, and I have to pick up a few night shifts. I'm pretty sure I can arrange something with the principals to rehearse during the day on the 19th. The chorus rehearsal on the fifth is the bigger problem. I think that'll have to be rescheduled."

He laughed in disbelief. "That's unacceptable. The accompanist does not set the rehearsal schedule."

"Oh, that's all right," Morgan said, making sure to smile. "I don't mind at all. I'm an expert at it."

"No, I mean, I don't want the schedule altered."

Toby, the production's music director, broke off a conversation with two of the chorus members and came over to listen.

Morgan shrugged. "OK. Maybe Toby would be able to sit in on the fifth."

Toby nodded, eager, his freckled face blushing a bit. She'd worked with him many times before. He didn't like confrontation. Unfortunately, he was an orchestral conductor, and his piano technique was minimalist and practical at best.

Charles glared at them both. "No. Absolutely not."

Morgan raised her eyebrows and wrinkled her forehead, feigning puzzlement. Then she relaxed her brow, giving up another, smaller shrug. "Then maybe Heritage Midwest can find a substitute. I'll contact the office tomorrow morning."

"That's unacceptable!" Charles said again, raising his voice. "This is a professional opera, not some penny-ante high school musical or dance recital."

Toby shook his head in alarm. "Really, Charles. One rehearsal is not a big deal."

Charles looked at him with pity for his weakness. Then he said to Morgan, "You'll be at all rehearsals, or you don't have a job!"

She exhaled, midway between a sigh and a huff. She wanted to tell him that what she did outside rehearsals was a hell of a lot more important to the rest of the world than his penny-ante production of *Peter Grimes*. But instead, she said, matter-of-fact and almost pleasant, "In that case, there are a lot more rehearsals you'll have to find an accompanist for." She looked him straight in the eye, watching his anger and pride grow to hide the incipient panic she was sure he felt.

"This is why I can't stand working with amateurs!" Charles spat out. "I can't believe you came so highly recommended."

"That's precisely why I'm highly recommended," Morgan said. "I don't do it for the money."

He leaned back a bit, surprised but not deterred. "If you can't muster up enough professionalism to give this production your highest priority, you're not a part of it!"

"OK," she said in a neutral voice. "That's your call, I guess. I'm still available as a répétiteur, as well as for almost all of the scheduled rehearsals." And she knew the music, she added silently. And she was good.

The room had become much quieter when Charles raised his voice. Ford was still at the piano, though, picking out buffoonish snippets from the opening Moot Hall scene. Charles said, "I'll see that you never work here again."

Morgan shouldered her bag. "Is my dismissal immediate, or would you prefer that I stay for rehearsal?"

Charles opened his mouth as if he wanted to yell and then closed it and turned away. "Like I have a choice!"

Ford piped up, "I'll be happy to play for rehearsal today."

Hopeful, Charles turned toward Ford but then realized he was being ridiculed. Morgan asked, "Wouldn't it mess up the blocking if Peter Grimes were seated at the piano the whole time?"

Ford laughed. Charles didn't.

Then Isabel entered. Oblivious to the scene that had just played out, she hurried straight to Morgan. "Hi—Morgan, isn't it? Do you have a minute before rehearsal? I'd like to schedule some sessions with you. You're available aren't you?"

Several people nearby started to laugh, and Isabel looked around, bewildered. "What's going on?" she asked with a hand on her hip and a frown between her eyes.

Isabel Dambrosio was a beautiful woman, 30ish or maybe a bit older, just heading into her prime—younger than Ellen Orford, the character she was playing. She had a dramatic stage presence that she wore most of the time, and the more envious among the sopranos called her "Callas," always with ironic inflection. She wore her long dark hair up and away from her face. Her eyes were dark too, rimmed with dark lashes and framed by thick dark brows plucked to perfection. Her olive skin was flawless, and she had a straight, regal nose that would serve her well in any number of disdainful operatic roles. She was not a Callas, though, not at all the type to blow out her voice. Nothing about this woman said reckless, once you got past her drop-dead beauty.

"What's going on?" she asked again.

Morgan checked Charles and saw him bending over his score, making a show of ignoring them. Toby was saying something to him and seemed to be ignored as well.

"Charles just blackballed me," Morgan said. "So your timing was kind of humorous, that's all."

Isabel thought a moment, trying to gauge the situation. "You don't look worried. Why'd he blackball you?"

"I have conflicts with a couple of rehearsals." She lowered her voice to a more confidential volume. "He backed himself into a corner trying to get his way, and he ended up firing me. I expect it'll all blow over."

Isabel raised her eyebrows and lowered her jaw a little.

"Anyway, if you'd like, we can arrange a few sessions," Morgan said.

Isabel looked away, mulling it over.

"Really, it's OK. Charles just needs to cool down. He won't retaliate." She laughed a little under her breath. "As long as you know your part. And if you don't, he'll probably blame me and not you. Ask Ford, if you're worried. Charles won't blackball both principals! And I'd love to work with you."

She nodded, cautious. "Ford recommended you." She looked at Morgan with suspicion but didn't ask a question. She glanced over at Ford, and Morgan saw him give her one of his most engaging smiles. So Ford was at work on Isabel, Morgan thought. That was predictable.

"All right," Charles said irritably, "let's get started."

Ford

I suppose there have been times when I've let my own ego get in the way of my best interests—seems to be an occupational hazard of musicians. I still laugh, though, when I see it happening to others. Morgan, of course, was unruffled. She knew Charles would come crawling back, though I think even she was surprised that it came so quickly. He apologized, so contrite, at the end of the rehearsal.

She was brilliant tonight. She can read a director so well—anticipate what he wants, whether parts or accompaniment, even a single phrase of a single line. She knew as well as Charles—no, better—what the singers needed to hear. Five minutes into the prologue, Charles had forgotten that his accompanist was a separate person who had a separate schedule.

Morgan was her typical gracious self as she accepted Charles' apology. That's purely professionalism on her part by the way. I know inside she was gloating, and I look forward to pulling it out of her next time I see her. But then, that might prove difficult. She's been more closed off than usual lately.

I first met Morgan almost 10 years ago, when I performed in an all-Monteverdi program of the Early Music Society. I'd just arrived at Wolverton State after 10 years in Europe. She was well known around the music school, this grad student in meteorology who was a fantastic accompanist. When I heard the harpsichord at the first Monteverdi rehearsal, I figured it had to be her—it was the best basso continuo I'd ever come across, and I've performed a lot of Renaissance and Baroque music. Morgan's articulation was so precise, her attacks were so intelligent—yet so inevitable that they defied calculation. And to think she wasn't even studying music.

It gave her a rare independence, that. She was her own musician—she had no fear. She never worried about losing future gigs or alienating someone she might need a recommendation from. Morgan never took any shit from anyone, whether instrumentalist, singer, or conductor. She handled everyone the way she handled Charles tonight. She might love music, but as far as any one gig was concerned, she could take it or leave it.

She felt the same way about me. It must be the lure of the unattainable, but even now, every time I see her I want to take those slender fingers and taste the tip of each one. So much beauty rests in those fingertips. I'd love to feel them on the nape of my neck, on the small of my back.

I wasn't quite that enamored of her yet when we were working on the Monteverdi, but I was definitely intrigued. After our first rehearsal, I slipped onto the bench next to her. She raised both eyebrows at me as she rose, so discreet, not too abruptly but still in a hurry. I played the tenor line of one of our pieces and she said, "Don't get too attached to those intervals. This instrument will have a different temperament in a few weeks."

"I'm flexible. Besides, playing my part was just an excuse to get close to you."

She snorted at that. A little snort, a cute snort. She squatted down, reaching to the floor for her bookbag, and she laid her left hand atop the music she had gathered on the bench. Hardly accidental, the placement of her hand. She was wearing an engagement ring.

I played another line from the tenor part. She said, "You're not a harpsichordist, are you?"

"No, I'm not. How can you tell?"

She smiled with confident condescension and shook her head.

"Articulation, right?"

She nodded, her surprised smile saying, OK, you've impressed me. As she stood up, just when she didn't need her left hand to balance anymore, I took it and looked closely at her ring. The diamond was small, just a chip, I'd say, though a nicely cut chip—I'll give Rob that much.

"That's a lovely ring," I said.

"Thank you," she said and tossed her hand out of mine. Just for a second, I saw the inside of her wrist. There were scars.

I have dreams about them sometimes, those scars. Wondering what they mean. Two thin white lines running three inches from her left wrist toward her elbow. Paler than her skin. She wears a wide watchband and long sleeves much of the time, so they're hardly noticeable. You almost have to be looking for them.

But somehow I caught a glimpse of them and noticed milky white painted on creamy ivory. Maybe I stared, following her hand as it drifted to her side. I looked at her face then, caught only her sharp profile. She was looking down, rooting through her bookbag. She had the half-smile that I would come to know as her habitual expression.

"What were those?" I asked.

"What?"

"The scars on your wrist."

"They're scars." I had clearly asked a supremely stupid question about the most obvious thing in the world.

"You tried to kill yourself?"

"No. I cut my wrist. Years ago now."

"So it was a pathetic cry for help."

"No, I wouldn't say so." She rested her right hand on the nameboard of the harpsichord and put her left hand behind her back. It was playful, almost like she was going to take a bow. But she was hiding the wrist, as if she knew I wanted another look and she was withholding it from me. Not because she minded my looking. No, it was just to deprive me of what I wanted. That's often the essence of Morgan's playfulness.

She leaned toward me, something like the bow I thought might be coming, and said, "I just wanted a little sleep."

She's never said anything more about it than that.

Three

The more Morgan worked with Isabel on *Peter Grimes*, the more she loved her voice. Isabel had a captivating lyric soprano that was liquid but still precise. Not sloppy at all. Morgan couldn't stand the constant gliding portamenti so many opera singers practiced. It was expected in the bel canto repertoire, and she'd heard soprano after soprano ruin some of Puccini's loveliest melodies with it. Isabel used it sparingly, almost never in her private sessions with Morgan. The logic behind Britten's harmonies was not always easy to discern, and Isabel was focused on getting the right notes above all else.

At the moment she was singing a beautiful aria that was by turns wistful and sinister. *Embroidery in childhood was a luxury of idleness.* Ellen sang this on finding a jersey she had embroidered for Peter's young apprentice, when she suspected something terrible had happened to the boy.

The sweetness of Isabel's voice carried both love and regret, a tempered longing for innocence and an awareness that it was lost forever. Too bad she couldn't get the right notes when Morgan played the accompaniment. Morgan stopped and shook her head.

"Are you sure you're playing the right notes?" Isabel asked, frowning.

Morgan tilted her head to the side and tried to give her a withering glare, but Isabel wasn't the withering type. So she said, "Yes. That's my job. And you're making it harder for us both by doubting me."

Isabel pursed her lips and looked down, trying to muster some trust in her répétiteur. Her hair was up and away from her face, and the angle of her head was dramatic, all the right tendons in her neck stretched to elegant effect. In profile she reminded Morgan of a Victorian cameo, silhouetted against the white background of the studio wall.

"It shouldn't be that difficult," Isabel said. "And it wouldn't be if Britten didn't distract you—I don't know why he had to give the orchestra so many weird chords."

"Well, I guess it was because he was a genius." Morgan grinned, and Isabel's face relaxed. "It's about simplicity that's complicated by circumstances—the simple pleasure of embroidery comes back as a clue to the cruelty of the man she loves. It's not simple."

Isabel nodded, and they began again.

"Watch that C–double sharp," Morgan interrupted and played the interval.

"Why the hell can't he just make it a D?"

"You really don't want to know." Morgan tossed a pencil to her, which Isabel caught on reflex, though she was startled. "Go ahead and mark it a D because it's hard enough to find with the accompaniment. I'm playing a D-sharp. Listen to the line, and just learn it as a tune for now." She played two bars alone, and Isabel repeated them back to her. "Again." Isabel repeated the line without Morgan playing. "Good!"

A door whispered open opposite the baby grand Morgan was playing, and a girl slipped into the room. She had curly dark hair that was unruly in a charming tomboy kind of way, and she had a rather uncharming frown. She had a gym bag slung over her shoulder, and she slumped into a chair in the far corner as if she belonged there. She looked about 12.

Isabel was oblivious to the intruder, and she finished out the phrase. Morgan stopped and said to the girl, "Can we help you?"

"I doubt it," the girl said.

"Emilia!" Isabel admonished. "You be more polite, girl." To Morgan she said, "It's my daughter. I asked her to meet me here. I was able to get her some gymnastics lessons over at the Y that end at 11:30. Just pretend she isn't here."

Morgan hesitated, then said, "I generally don't allow children at rehearsals." Emilia's frown deepened, and she huffed in much the same way Isabel did. Maybe she didn't like being called a child. Maybe she was older than Morgan thought. She could be 16 for all Morgan knew.

"It's only for another half hour," Isabel said. She didn't hide her annoyance.

"Can you behave that long?" Morgan asked Emilia.

"Of course she can," Isabel answered with a severe look in Emilia's direction. Morgan looked again at Emilia. "I said, she'll behave," Isabel insisted. "Let's get on with it."

"Since Emilia's the one who has to behave, I'd like to know that she concurs."

Emilia's mouth twitched a little in amusement, and her thick eyebrows separated. "Yeah. Sure, I concur." She snickered a little. "It's not like I've got ADHD."

Morgan froze for a split second, then said, "I'm glad to hear it," forcing her breath and a smile. "So let's get on with it. 'Embroidery in childhood,' pickup to 23."

Isabel's singing was heavier with Emilia in the room, and Morgan had the impression she meant to sound older, more powerful. "Lighten up your tone," Morgan said without stopping. Isabel frowned and kept on singing, lightening up some. "More," Morgan said, "think young and innocent."

"But she's not young and innocent," Isabel countered at the end of the phrase in which she had sung every note correctly.

"You got the C–double sharp. Good." Morgan stopped playing. "She may not be young, but I think you have to see her as innocent or at least as pretty naïve, unless you want her complicit in negligent homicide."

"For Pete's sake, it's an opera, not an episode of *Law & Order*."

Morgan felt herself bristle, and she strained to keep the irritation out of her voice with limited success. "This is not *The Magic Flute* either. There's supposed to be a semblance of realism. One boy has already died from Peter Grimes' neglect, yet she helped him get another apprentice. If she's as world-weary as you make her sound, it's hard to see her as a sympathetic character. Besides, you sound better without all that dark resonance in your sinuses."

Isabel pulled herself up to her full height, asserting her authority. "It's not your place to tell me how to develop the character. You're here to help me learn the notes."

"That's a poor use of your time and mine. As you might imagine, Charles doesn't tell me his innermost thoughts on character development, but I did play for the auditions, and I did hear him discussing the show with the production staff. He chose your voice because of its lightness. And he specifically said he liked the way it made you sound more innocent."

Emilia sat up, fascinated. Isabel was steaming. Morgan could tell she was about to boil over and was curious to see what words would come out of her mouth. But Isabel seemed not to be able to find words, or at least she couldn't speak them with Emilia present.

So Morgan went on. "If you want to get darker from this point on—that would be great actually. Here you realize something terrible has happened. You can't be naïve anymore. Save that darker, heavier tone for the latter part of 'my broidery affords a clue . . . whose meaning we avoid.' But go back to the lighter tone for the next verse—you're trying to recapture the innocence of childhood, but in the end, the clue is still in your hand—childhood innocence betrayed."

Isabel stepped around the curve of the baby grand and stood close to Morgan, towering over her. She said, *sotto voce*, "Don't criticize me in front of my daughter. I have a hard enough time getting a 13-year-old to mind, and I don't appreciate you being rude to me."

"I wasn't being rude," Morgan said, matching Isabel's low tone. She couldn't see Emilia now that Isabel was standing in front of her. "I was doing my job, and if you don't like it, find another répétiteur." Lowering her voice even more, she continued. "Your daughter will respect you more if she sees more give and take in your dealings with other people. And you'd certainly be a better role model for her."

"You obviously don't have children."

Morgan felt a spasm in her back. "No, I don't," she whispered. Then she slammed her score shut, stuffed it into her portfolio, and slid the bench out from the piano with a loud scrape. Isabel's eyes widened in surprise, and Morgan stood up. She said in her normal voice, "I think we both can see that the session went better without Emilia here." She stepped away from the piano and pushed the bench toward it. "You have my number if you want to schedule another."

Isabel stood with her mouth open for a few seconds before saying, "I'll be sure to tell Heritage Midwest not to pay you for the last half hour."

"And I'll be sure to tell them why the session ended early."

Isabel looked frightened for two seconds and then regained her composure. Emilia appeared fascinated with this interchange. Morgan stopped and decided to be merciful. "OK, I'll just report an hour session rather than ninety minutes."

Isabel sighed and glanced again at Emilia, who now had a smirk on her face. Morgan turned to the door and, as she opened it, said under her breath, "I asked the wrong person if she'd behave." She heard Emilia laugh as the door shut.

That might cause some trouble, Morgan thought, and an old uneasiness settled on her.

*   *   *

When Morgan was 26 and finishing up her master's in meteorology, she had taken a continuo gig with the Early Music Society for a concert of Monteverdi. It was early spring, and the weather had taken a sudden balmy turn, wreaking havoc with the harpsichord's tuning. The society rehearsed in the university's Renaissance Hall, and as the musicians straggled in, the room's live acoustics magnified the murmured greetings, the click of locks on instrument cases, and the scraping of chairs and metal stands across the floor. Morgan held her hair back from her forehead, sounded an F-sharp octave, and forced herself to focus on the pitches. The beats came fast and furious. They needed much better environmental controls in this room. She steadied her elbow against the nameboard and placed the tuning hammer on the pin.

The harpsichord lurched beneath her so suddenly she lost her balance.

"Hi, Morgan!" a little girl yelled as she bounced up against her, bubbling over with laughter and recklessness.

"Callie!" Morgan scolded. "You just can't do that!" She picked herself up off the harpsichord bench she'd stumbled onto. "Oh, shit! Would you look at that? The tuning pin's bent. Just look at what you did!"

"Where? Where?" Callie couldn't look at it, in fact, as her six-year-old body wasn't yet four feet tall, but she nevertheless grabbed the harpsichord and bounced up on her toes, trying to see inside.

"Oh, just stop it, would you?" Morgan hissed. "You have to be careful around these instruments. They're delicate."

Callie threw herself a few steps back from the harpsichord and scowled. The girl was like an erratic storm system that never quite blew itself out.

Her dark eyes were loaded with tears and Morgan could feel the pressure dropping. Next might be a temper tantrum or a violent paroxysm of grief. Morgan squatted down and brushed a few stringy strands of brown hair behind the girl's ears. "Callie," she said, trying to be sympathetic, "you're just getting too big to throw yourself around like that. You won't just hurt things, you'll end up hurting people, too."

"I didn't hurt the harpsword!" she protested. "There's no bumps on it."

"Callie!" Jana, Callie's always exasperated mother, towered over them. "What did you get into this time?"

"Nothing!" Callie tore away across the rehearsal room, two black music stands clattering over in her wake.

Jana set her viola da gamba case down with care, then exhaled. "I don't know what to do with that girl." Jana was tall and bony, with long brown hair that she never did anything with but flip over her shoulder.

Morgan straightened up and looked at Jana looking at Callie. "No luck finding a sitter?"

Jana gave Morgan a dead sarcastic look. "My mother won't even take her anymore!" She was only a year or two older than Morgan, but she looked a lot closer to 40.

It surprised Morgan that she had so much more tolerance for Callie than most other people did. Sometimes she thought she was trying to understand the rules behind Callie's behavior so she could track it, like a mesocyclone. "She's just a vacuum for attention, that one," Morgan said. She and Jana looked at Callie trying to talk to one of the crumhorn players.

Jana frowned, and her dark brown eyes widened a bit, guilt-ridden. They were the only part of her that looked like Callie, who was round and pudgy with what would've been called baby fat in a younger child. "It might help if Kyle would ever take a turn," she said. "But, no, he's too busy laying the foundation for his career to pay any attention to his daughter. Some career. What are the chances he'll sing at the Met? About the same as me playing Carnegie Hall."

The bitterness and guilt in Jana's voice gave Morgan a chill, but it was nothing new. Jana and her husband, both overextended graduate students, had always had a difficult relationship.

"Callie didn't do any major damage, did she?" Jana asked, flipping her hair over her shoulder with a resolute twist of her head.

"No, she just made me bend a tuning pin. It'll be OK—just take a while for the pitch to stabilize, is all." They were both looking inside the harpsichord now. "See—that F-sharp on the front eight-foot. I might be able to straighten it out by next week. With all this humidity streaming up from the south lately, I'll have to keep tuning it up anyway, so it's no big deal."

Jana laughed. "I'm surprised more harpsichordists don't become meteorologists, the way these instruments react to the weather."

"I am too actually."

"So give me some good news. Is spring really here? I mean, can I put away my down jacket for good?"

Morgan snorted. "In early March? This is the Midwest—it might be 50 degrees today. In a few days it might even be 70—but we'll get at least one more arctic blast from Canada that'll dry out all this humidity and land us all in the deep freeze for a week." Morgan had seen some indications of just that on the computer models earlier that day. "And you know what that means."

Jana shook her head.

"The bass strings will go sharp and the high treble flat, and I'll be spending more time tuning than playing."

"Jana!" The director's nasal tenor cut through the general noise of tuning and warm-ups, harsh with irritation. "Would you keep this little hellion away from my music!" He was picking up some loose pages off the floor. Callie was jumping around behind him, laughing. "I'm warning you, Jana. I don't care if the concert is in two weeks, you're out if you can't keep your kid under control."

Morgan caught the look on Jana's face—eyes narrowed, spots of red over her angular cheekbones, lips parted in disgust—and another deep chill ran through her.

Jana strode across the rehearsal room toward her daughter. "Callie! I am at the end of my rope! Do you want to die?" Callie's eyes got very big before she turned and ran out into the corridor.

The chill didn't leave Morgan for the rest of that evening.

*   *   *

Ten years later, Morgan was remembering the father who had given her so much love and attention as she was growing up. Her eyes filled with tears. He had somehow been a great dad while also being a great artist. How did he manage that? Especially after Mom had died. Morgan felt so inadequate, not being able to figure that out.

She didn't like feeling inadequate, so she focused harder on the radar screen in front of her and adjusted the colors to actual. Black and gray twisted about themselves in a slow dance of tone and texture. There were fine cracks of yellow and gray-green khaki, very muted, barely perceptible, but Morgan had a keen eye for such gradations. It was her job, and she was good at it.

This was not a storm you would want to experience first-hand. These were elements to avoid. She adjusted the screen again, zoomed in to examine finer microscale features, and the red began to emerge, like rose petals. The way they caught the light, the images just had to be three-dimensional, but Morgan knew very well they were not. She marveled at the fidelity of the computer screen. Had they upgraded the resolution without telling her? How could she have missed that? But there they were, scarlet rose petals swirling in the black and gray storm. She had to find out where they were going. Had to find out where they would land. At this point, she didn't even know if the petals were floating up or down or what forces were pulling at them. She was aware of a faint odor—something evocative, terrible and evocative. Suddenly she wasn't sure whether the black storm was meteorological. It could be subatomic, the computer monitor streaming video from an electron microscope with Dad at the controls, choosing the colors, still waiting for the right moment to snap the picture.

She needed more data. Should she call a weather spotter? She checked the coordinates on the radar image. Maybe a look out the window would be all she needed. The window seemed to be in a strange place, around a corner in the operations area she hadn't been aware of before. The light streaming in was gray as if it were either dusk or very cloudy. She left the computer with some trepidation and stood before a wide double-sashed window. The storm was indeed meteorological. It was swirling outside.

She opened the window, and the evocative odor flowed in. It was very familiar: linseed oil. So this was one of Dad's paintings. But the swirling currents of the storm were out of kilter, tiny eddies breaking out where there should have been a strong smooth line. The trees! She had forgotten to compensate for the trees! The storm was passing too close to the ground, and now she saw it—petals were getting caught in the treetops, shredded by the uppermost twigs. This was a disaster—Dad's painting was being destroyed! Now she understood her job, but it was too late.

She felt the strange oily air encase her arms and face and pull her out of the window. She wondered what this strange fluid medium was—not air but breathable, not water but swimmable. She frog-kicked to the treetops, and she unwrapped a petal larger than her head from a mess of twigs. It broke her heart to see it float away damaged. Why did Dad let this happen? Why had he left her without any instructions? The wind bent as it swirled toward the gray light source near the horizon or near where Morgan thought the horizon might be. Why did it bend? The Coriolis effect? Or was it some weird permutation of the wave theory? Was this light she was dealing with? Another petal that was caught on the tree limbs broke free and was carried away in tatters.

"No, that's all wrong!" Morgan tried to yell, but the oily medium around her didn't carry sound, and the sound waves built up in her throat until the pain was intolerable and she couldn't breathe. She should never have tried to speak.

Morgan woke up with a start and recognized the stucco ceiling of the bedroom, plaster points casting tiny spiked shadows in the blue gray light from the window. She relaxed her throat and took a deep breath to calm the roiling thunderheads in her chest. She still smelled linseed oil.

She rubbed tears out of her eyes and threw the covers off, welcoming the rush of cold dry air, which banished the vestiges of sleep. It was Saturday morning, and she stuffed her feet into her fleece slippers, hugged her green flannel pajamas around her, and made her way to the living room. She looked at the low table where they kept Dad's paints and saw the box was missing.

She couldn't believe it. Rob had no idea what he was doing.

She walked around the stairs and saw Rob in front of the bay window with one of Dad's old easels—the smallest one, with the roller on one leg that always stuck. He'd set it up on an old drop cloth he must have gotten out of the garage. She couldn't see what he was working on, but she could see him. He glanced up at her with an embarrassed smile, a smile that begged indulgence.

"Surprised?" He laughed a little. "I just spent an hour cleaning and oiling that one roller that never worked. Nothing like procrastination to get odd jobs done, huh?"

He was looking now at whatever was on the easel, not at her. She wanted to slap him.

"What the hell do you think you're doing?" Her voice was low and menacing.

Rob was bewildered. "Painting?"

Morgan moved to the other side of the easel and looked. There she saw a piece of canvas board, barely bigger than a sheet of notebook paper. At least he wasn't using Dad's supply of canvas. He had a few lines stroked in. Cobalt. She couldn't tell what he was going for yet. He had a black and white photograph of some geosynthetic material pinned to the top of the easel.

"You're not a painter," she said almost in a whisper.

"I've put some paint on canvas." She could hear the resolve in his voice. He wasn't going to back down. "Or on canvas board anyway. So that makes me a painter, at least in Dad's eyes."

She did slap him. His cheek felt rough and stung her hand. He put down Dad's palette and paintbrush on a small collapsible table he had retrieved from the basement. He rubbed the spot where she had slapped him. No real damage done. She regretted that and wondered whether she should try again.

He said, his voice very low, "That was unnecessary."

She shook out her hand and stared at the fresh paint smeared on Dad's palette. They stood there for a long moment, not moving, and not looking at each other.

"Why did you do that?" he finally asked.

"Don't you ever tell me what my Dad thinks. And you have no right to use his paints." She wanted to throw his little canvas board into the bay window, shatter the glass and clear the smell out of the house.

"He gave them to me." He stood between the easel and Morgan, demanding her attention. She stared into his T-shirted chest. "Me. Not you."

"Thanks for rubbing my nose in it."

"You're welcome, but that's not what I'm doing. He wanted me to paint. He's been bugging me to start using oils for two years—so have you! How many times have you said, 'I'd love to see what you can do in a liquid medium'? I thought you'd be happy that I'm finally going for it."

She looked at him, furious. His eyes were cold, glittery. "Why should I be happy about you destroying something that belongs to my Dad? It's all I have left of him."

"Give me a break, Morgan! He left you his paintings, you have his piano. You have a lifetime of memories besides. This is not something you need to keep. He always said, 'Paint on the canvas is always better than paint in the tube.'"

She would've slapped him again, but he caught her hand on the way to his face.

"You're a lot stronger than you look." Tears were welling up in his eyes, and he wasn't trying to hold them back.

Good. She was glad he was hurt. She wanted him to let go of her hand so she could slap him again.

"I miss him too," he said, searching her face. "But are we all just supposed to stand still?"

"He's my father."

"Fine. Your father. Fine." He let go of her hand and turned away.

Hitting his back wouldn't be as satisfying as slapping his face again.

"Can't you think of anyone but yourself?" he asked. "Dad belongs to a lot more people than you. He had students, colleagues. He had us, his family. I was part of his family. If you try to tell me I wasn't, then you're just deluded." He picked up his canvas board and faced her again, shaking his head as if he didn't know what to say. "What the hell is wrong with you, Morgan? You deny yourself what you love and then feel sorry for yourself because you don't have it!"

She was not feeling sorry for herself. Whatever she denied herself was denied for good reasons. "You don't know what the hell you're talking about."

"Then explain it to me. Why don't you play anymore?"

"What does that have to do with anything?" She was losing control of her decibel level. She lowered her voice back to menacing. "I play piano all the time."

"You don't play piano, you work the piano. It's all work. Practice, discipline."

"Oh—and there's something wrong with discipline?"

"No. It lets us both get a lot done. But what good is it if you don't enjoy anything? You're just hoarding things now." He unpinned the photo from the easel. "Well, keep me out of your dog-in-the-manger world. Take the damned paints and the brushes and the easel. If I knew how, I'd make that stupid roller stick again for you. Put it all back safe the way it was. Keep it pure."

That word knocked all other words out of her mind.

"And keep your grief pure while you're at it. Keep it all as pure as your bitter self. But don't expect me to be happy about it." He stepped around her and headed toward his basement office. When he reached the basement door, he stopped and said, "I really am more of an artist than you are right now." He lifted his pathetic canvas board. "Here's the proof."

She wanted to throw something at him, but the only things at hand were Dad's. So she just screamed at him instead.

He looked surprised and even pleased with himself. He actually smiled as he opened the door.

Morgan shook out her right hand again and looked at it this time. It had stopped stinging, but it was red. She wiggled all the fingers, and they worked OK. Then she balled them up into a fist.

Rob

Of course it didn't hurt me physically. The sting was gone in a few seconds. But the emotional sting is still here a week later, and I'm still thinking about it. Because she wasn't sorry, and I don't think she's sorry yet.

In the 12 years we've been together, she has never done anything like that. She's the kind of person who takes pride in being cool and calm when she's angry. I've always thought of her anger as an endothermic system, gathering heat, leaving the person she's angry with out in the cold. If it's me she's angry with, giving her more heat just freezes me out more effectively. I have learned to reason with her until her heat turns to light and we reach an understanding, and I've always admired the way she insists on that approach. It works. When we argue, we get something accomplished. But when all of a sudden she goes exothermic and lashes out, what am I supposed to do? Maybe giving her more heat was good. At least I got her to scream. I've been thinking she might need more of that.

It's just so out of character for her. Slapping me. Screaming. And sneering at my painting too—she's always loved it when I sketch and draw! There's this little cafe where we used to go on Saturday mornings before Dad died. We'd get a scone or a muffin and a cappuccino or latte and plan out the week, talk about what we were looking forward to or sometimes what we were dreading. And we'd talk about the art on the walls of the cafe.

Morgan used to say, "Your pastels are so much better than these paintings"—or photographs or etchings or monotypes. "I could really see your work up there on these walls."

I don't think I'm good enough though. Sure, I have some things that are better than some of the stuff the cafe puts up, but it doesn't touch the best of what I've seen there.

For my birthday last year, Morgan had one of my pastels matted and framed. She thought I could put it up in my office on campus, but I put it up in our bedroom. She keeps on wanting me—or she used to keep wanting me—to show my stuff to more people, like to my colleagues. It's not ready though. That's how I feel. It's not ready. It's like submitting a research article before all the data is in, before I get a chance to analyze it. The big picture could change dramatically.

"So what?" Morgan says (about art, not about research). "That's the thing about art. It might change, but that doesn't necessarily mean that the earlier version is better or worse."

That was Dad talking, I think. He's said similar things to me over the years. But he understood my not wanting to show my work. He told me once, "There's definitely a point when you feel something is ready to be public. Don't push it. But still, get private opinions—ask other artists, friends. Or family." He smiled and gave me one of those half hugs around the shoulders.

The last time Morgan suggested I try to get the cafe to display some of my pastels, I reminded her of what Dad said.

"Oh, Dad!" she said, with a mock roll of the eyes. "He doesn't understand you engineers, always wanting to make sure the wheels won't fall off. The point is if the wheels fall off it's still art. Engineers need a push."

She said that with a smile. And then she gave me the look.

I wonder if I'll ever see the look again. Right now it's almost like she wants me to be as angry with her as she is with me.

But I don't want to be angry with her. I want to talk to her, laugh with her, put my arms around her and hear her whisper in my ear. Have a life together. It doesn't have to be the life we had before Dad died, but let's have some enjoyment or sadness or something that's not anger, something that doesn't give me this raging heartburn!

I just don't know how to fix this because I don't know why she's so mad at me.

She shows no interest in what I'm doing, and I'll be damned if I'm going to ask her what she thinks about it. I try to ask her how the opera's going, try to joke about Ford like we used to, but her answers are short and without any of her normal enthusiasm. I mention that Tracy came by making more woeful complaints about being a stay-at-home mom, and she frowns and doesn't reply. Sometimes she even walks out of the room. About all we can find to talk about is the weather and our schedules, which might keep us connected, but it doesn't get us anywhere. I guess it's easier than talking about my derailed research or Dad or painting. Or the fact that she slapped me and wasn't one bit sorry about it.

So I sit down in the basement using pastels to sketch out the paintings I'd like to work on, while she putters around the place, tuning up the generator out back, changing light bulbs, checking the furnace filter, putting a load of wash through. She never looks over my shoulder as I draw anymore, never slips her arms around my neck like she used to. She just goes upstairs and works on *Peter Grimes*—always on the Steinway, never upstairs at the piano in her music studio.

How come she gets to play Dad's piano, but I can't use his paints? Hell, I'm afraid to even touch the damn paint box. She's stashed it away in her studio closet now anyway, where she keeps his smaller paintings and all his supplies. Stashed away in the least-used part of her life.

Well, that's the long and short of why I've set up an easel here in my office. I've bought my own set of oils and brushes, a new drop cloth, but I couldn't bring myself to try again at home. I don't want to subject myself to any more of her sneering, not until I feel more confident in what I want to do.

This is unusual equipment to see in a civil engineer's office. Even drafting boards are rare anymore! But I figure, hey, I've got tenure. It's about time I developed some eccentricities.

Still, I felt a jolt when Walter Taney stopped in just now. He's the chair of our department, and sure, I know the guy, but we don't exactly run in the same circles. He tapped on the door and stuck his head in, asking if I knew what the strange smell out in the hall was.

"Oh, no, it's not unpleasant," he said. "Not at all. It's just unfamiliar. Linseed oil, you said?" He chuckled as he stepped into the office. "Oh, yes. This is definitely the smell. Well, as long as it's not some toxic leak from one of the chem labs."

He liked the painting I'm working on. It's based on a soil sample map and some visual climatic data that I've been having some problems analyzing. I laid the outline of a section out using a hard pencil on the canvas and then used color to make parts of it glow. I ended up shifting some of the features around to balance them out. Walter didn't recognize it as a map at first, but he loved the idea when I explained what I was doing. He was disappointed when I told him my painting muse didn't seem to be in cahoots with my engineering muse, and I had resolved none of the problems of the actual analysis. Not yet anyway.

"Well then," he said, "live in hope!"

This canvas board is only eleven by fourteen inches, a size I'm fond of right now. Manageable. I remember a few years ago Dad was urging me to break out of my small sketchbooks. I had just started working in pastels. He wanted me to conceive broader compositions, using three large sheets of drawing paper. But somehow, they always turned into triptychs rather than single pieces—unsuccessful triptychs at that. Each panel worked better apart from the others.

"You know, Rob," he said as he examined my last triptych in his studio. "You're a small surface artist. At least right now. Next time I tell you you have to work like me, just tell me to stop being such a control freak. You be your own artist."

He meant a lot to me.

And I meant a lot to him. Just last year, he'd dipped his brush in cobalt blue and handed it to me. "Here, Rob," he said, "put a few strokes on an immortal Jon Tallis." His clear blue eyes dared me. "See what you can do."

It was an abstract work, of course, medium size for him, maybe four by five feet. It had a lot of fuchsia and ochre in it. A combination I never would've put together, but it was working pretty well for him. The cobalt was over the top though—that's what I was thinking. But I took a deep breath and added a dot to a circular form in the upper left, as if it were a reflection on a bubble. I heard Dad inhale like he was about to say something, but I had more to do. I put a few quick strokes along a narrow straight line that was broken by a slash of black, as if the line had been struck by the same blue light as the bubble and the black slash was the shadow. Only then did I look at Dad. He seemed so surprised! In a good way, like I'd done a whole lot better than he'd expected.

"That's really interesting," he said. "Good! I'm leaving it there."

"Here I thought you'd be stuck with what I did."

He laughed. "Nothing's ever final, Rob. As long as you have paint left."

That painting was among the finished works we found after he'd died, and he did leave my brushstrokes untouched. He added very little cobalt beyond that, but he called it *Cold Light*. When I saw it there in his studio, I cried. Morgan took my hand and squeezed it in that way she has, that active way, like a slow pulse. She was crying too.

I pointed to the blue strokes and said, "I put those there a few months ago. He handed me the brush with cobalt on it and said, see what you can do. He left them in."

Her hand froze, and when I looked at her, she was looking at the painting. There was something like anger and disbelief on her face. As if I had contaminated the painting.

I let go of her hand and took a Kleenex out of my pocket. "It's not like he couldn't paint over it if he didn't like it."

She looked away from the painting and at my face. The anger shifted to surprise, and then she looked away again. Lost.

I know she's hurting, but I don't know why she's shutting me out. And I don't know why I'm not allowed to be part of Dad's memory when I was part of his life.

Four

Morgan yawned and filled her coffee mug in the break room of the forecast office. High pressure was in control of the entire forecast region, as well as points north and west, into Canada and past the foothills of the Rockies 1,000 miles away. A huge mass of dry arctic air was sitting over the midsection of North America, not going anywhere in the next 12 hours at least. The jet stream was running a typical course for late winter in a non–El Niño year, and the ridge far to their west would give way only slowly to the trough behind it. In other words, the weather would be tediously predictable for the next 72 hours. Lots of sun and very little warmth with perfect conditions for radiational cooling at night. The snow and ice wouldn't be melting anytime soon, which was not so unusual for February but discouraging nevertheless.

Morgan watched as Susan navigated her pregnant self through the tight space around the break room table and opened the refrigerator. She took a big tub of yogurt out and dumped a packet of salted peanuts into it. Morgan envied her appetite. She took a sip of strong coffee and stared at the bulletin board over the counter.

"So what's with you, Morgan?"

"Huh?"

"That's the third big sigh you've let out in the past 15 minutes."

"You must be as bored as I am if you're counting my sighs."

"No, I'm just a natural-born multitasker." Susan stirred the peanuts into the yogurt. "What are you playing?"

Morgan looked down at her right hand and saw that indeed her fingers were playing something on the edge of the counter. She checked to see what piece was running through her mind. "It's something from that opera I've been accompanying. An aria Peter Grimes sings about the life he'd lead with the woman he loves if he had the money." She sang, none too sweetly, but on-key and with clear enunciation: "*Seen in stars the life we'd share, Fruit in the garden, children by the shore.*"

"Ah, how idyllic. But personally, I'd worry the kids would drown."

"You're not too far off the mark." In her mind's eye, Morgan saw a boy fall screaming from a cliff above the sea. She shuddered. "Not too much later in that scene, a little boy dies. It's a pretty disturbing opera if you ask me."

Susan, who had a strong and active five-year-old son at home, chewed a spoonful of peanuts and yogurt blissfully. She wasn't thinking too hard of drowning children.

"You ever worry about Luke drowning?"

"Sure, if we go to the beach," she said, placid enough. "Or to someplace where there's a pool." She laughed. "Bart actually suggested we get a pool a couple years ago when we had that extended heat wave. I don't know if he was just trying to get my goat or if he really was out of his mind. I tell you what—if he took a turn looking after Luke some afternoon, he'd see just how hard it is to keep that boy from hurting himself."

"I don't know how you do it," Morgan said, feeling the truth of it. "Sometimes I think if people aren't crazy in the first place for having a family, then all that responsibility will drive them crazy in the end."

"Sometimes you do go crazy. There just aren't enough hours in the day to get everything done that needs to be done—and I mean *needs* to be done. And then sometimes the day just won't *end*, and all you want is to crawl into bed for a few hours." Susan smiled. "They're worth it, though, kids. No matter how much trouble they are."

Morgan smiled, more out of politeness than agreement, and turned to head back into the operations area.

"You and Rob thinking of starting a family?"

"God, no!" Morgan felt her hair standing on end, as if lightning were about to strike. "Do you think we're crazy?"

Susan put a hand on her hip and frowned. "Sane people have been known to have kids, you know."

"I know, I know." Morgan tried to laugh. "It just took me off-guard. The question, I mean. Rob and I decided a long time ago that a family wasn't in the cards for us."

"I know, it's just that people sometimes think differently about family when they lose someone close." She was looking down into her yogurt but looked up all of a sudden as if hoping she hadn't said something wrong.

Morgan looked away, eyes stinging. "My dad always said you don't have kids just so they can carry on." She coughed. "That was his way of saying it was OK with him that we decided not to have a family. His work was his legacy."

"I always thought you guys would be good parents though."

Morgan shook her head. "Not with our schedules, we wouldn't."

"You're a whiz with schedules. You'd work it out if you wanted to."

"That's the thing—if we wanted to." And they didn't. "Nothing's ever simple, as any scheduling whiz can tell you. If you add something to the schedule, something else has to go. We're just not willing to make the sacrifices."

Susan looked sad for a moment. "You're right, I guess. But it's a shame. Don't you ever get baby pangs?"

"Baby pangs?"

"You know, you see a baby and you want one so bad it hurts."

"No, can't say I've ever experienced that." Morgan felt uncomfortable with that answer, like she was telling a lie. But she wasn't. "I'm more likely to feel I want children when I'm talking to older kids, like once they're in school. But wanting one so much that it hurts?" That just seemed strange. But familiar too. "You actually feel pain?"

"I'm pregnant," Susan laughed. "I feel pain all the time. But before I got pregnant the first time, yeah, I'd see a baby and just want to pick it up and hold it, and if I couldn't, my hands and feet would start to, I don't know, tingle, and my heart raced, and I felt like I was going to cry. Yeah. I felt some pain. But more like a pang."

Morgan saw herself upstairs in her house. In the music studio. Placing Dad's paintings in the cleared-out closet. The harpsichord behind her. And she felt herself afraid to look at the harpsichord. Knowing it was there. And knowing too that Rob was downstairs, wanting to help.

Morgan shook her head. "Maybe I have felt that way." It did seem familiar. "Not about babies though. I'm pretty sure of that."

*   *   *

Ten years before, when Morgan had been in graduate school and not yet married, a stretch of mild weather a week before the vernal equinox had infected just about everyone with spring fever. But Morgan felt cold in spite of the bright sunshine outside. A stiff wind blew from the west, seeping through the loose single-glazed windows into the living room of the old apartment she shared with Rob. Morgan pulled a sweater around herself and watched on her computer screen as heat from a nascent thunderstorm blossomed red over Hispaniola. She found it soothing to see the chaos of innumerable alternatives resolve into specific, definable weather.

She was trying not to think about Callie, the six-year-old who had no business being at the Early Music Society's rehearsals. But she couldn't help seeing the girl as a wolf, the leftover interval of her parents' life, squeezed out of tune and out of control by the time her parents spent on jobs, studies, music. Change the temperament, Morgan wanted to tell Jana—there must be others to choose from, some more well-tempered system. But Morgan couldn't figure out what that system might be, and she knew besides that it wasn't her business.

She heard Rob shuffle behind her into the kitchen and open the refrigerator door. "Cold today?" he asked.

"That's the general idea of a refrigerator."

"Are *you* cold today?" he corrected himself with a small laugh.

"It's the wind more than the temperature. Around 25 miles an hour, gusts to 35. Actually, I think there have been a few close to 40, but I haven't been near an anemometer today, so that's just a guess."

He closed the refrigerator. "You know, I really do admire your exactness, even when it's not to the point. Does that mean there's something wrong with me?"

"I think so. I do it to annoy you." She knew very well that he could beat her in any hair-splitting contest where he applied himself. But she also knew he didn't have much interest in splitting hairs.

"What are you looking at?" He leaned against her computer table with a cup of light coffee in his hand.

"Infrared images of the Caribbean," she said, looking up at him, wondering whether he would crumple the report he was half-sitting on. "You can see the thermals as the sun warms up the islands."

"Nothing's bothering you?"

"Why do you ask?"

He shrugged and looked toward the window. "You look at satellite images when something's bothering you."

"Or satellite images of the tropics when I'm cold."

"I'm told it's the wind more than the temperature, so I just thought I'd ask." He looked back at her, not quite smiling, and ran his warm hand behind her neck. She tipped her head back slightly, hoping he would rub a bit. But he took his hand away after the briefest of squeezes. The satellite feed had reached the present and abruptly started over from 24 hours earlier.

"You know Callie?" Morgan asked.

He narrowed his eyes and shook his head. Then he stopped and smiled. "Little girl, neglected daughter of a gamba player and a tenor who are always bickering."

Morgan knew he wasn't smiling at the information, just at the fact he had located it. She felt a quick surge of affection for him. "She was being a pest last night, and the director threatened to kick Jana out of the group. The look on her face—I guess that's what's bothering me."

"The look on Jana's face?"

"And her tone of voice. Desperate." She slowed down the satellite feed with a few clicks of the mouse to linger over a developing cluster of thunderstorms on the Yucatan.

"You know," Rob said, "nobody has all the time they need to be perfect parents, and even if they did, they'd still mess up." He took a sip of coffee. "Kids are durable. So are parents."

"Maybe." The heat from the thunderstorms blotted out the outline of the peninsula and spilled into the sea. "It's just that I understand how Jana feels. It's like Callie's threatening what she loves." Instead of being what she loves. Morgan wondered whether she should say what she was thinking when she found herself saying it. "Sometimes I think I'd feel the same way."

Rob stopped his mug halfway to his lips, then set it down on the desk. He didn't say anything for a few moments. More pockets of heat rose over western Cuba, and soon that half of the island was obscured. "Growing up," he said at last, "I always expected that I'd have kids someday. It just seemed like something that happens to everyone."

"That's what I thought too." She wanted to look at him, but she could only manage to look at his coffee mug.

"People find ways to make it work."

"Like taking your kids to a rehearsal because you can't find a sitter for the little hellions?" Wind shear carried away the tops of the storm cells over the open sea, prefiguring their decay. "Sometimes it just doesn't work."

"Think *we'd* have hellions?"

She felt his eyes searching for hers. She turned from the computer screen and almost met them. "With you at the lab all day and every other evening and me working overtime at some weather station and then rehearsing or performing after hours—you think we *wouldn't* have hellions?" Morgan grabbed the mouse and began to shut the application down. "That's Callie's problem. No one pays any attention to her. There's just not enough time for everyone to get what they want. One of the many flaws of the universe, I guess."

"So," he said, "you're thinking you don't want kids?"

She lifted her head and looked at his face. There were the beginnings of crow's feet at the corners of his eyes, and she imagined what he would look like 10, 20 years from now—lines in his face, gray salting his curly hair, the intelligence in his eyes even more thoughtful. All the cold tension she'd been carrying in her chest melted. She didn't want to take anything away from Rob—he should have children, as many as he wanted.

"I'm just thinking," she said and tried to smile. "It just feels like something bad is going to happen to Callie. Or Jana. I feel like I'm watching a supercell form on radar, and I can't get a warning out."

"It's not your job to forecast the path of other people's lives." He touched her face and smiled.

"Thank God for that. People don't even listen to weather reports."

"Well I do," he said and then kissed her. "And I'll even listen to your forecast of my life."

She laughed. "I notice you don't promise to believe it."

*   *   *

It was approaching 6 p.m. at the Richfield National Weather Service forecasting office when Morgan and Susan returned from the break room. Terence was just slipping into his coat. He was late heading home—some kind of conference call with a couple of NOAA officials on the West Coast had held him up. This was one of Morgan's swing shifts, and she and Susan would be working until midnight, as would Jack, who right now was preparing to go outside to launch the zero-hour UTC radiosonde into the star-filled sky. He put on a wool cap and zipped up his down parka and then was gone out the back door.

Nothing had changed on Morgan's computer screen at the short-term forecast work station. The screen was free of radar echoes, blank except for the outlines of counties she could see with her eyes closed. At least now she was pretty sure her eyes were open. She took another sip of coffee.

Weather was supposed to be ever-changing. When it stood still like this, it made her impatient. But today it was more than impatience. She felt disappointed, like a friend had let her down.

Figuring she might as well work on some training materials she had to get together for next week, she turned to another computer and began to adjust some graphics to illustrate the various prospects for precipitation when the vertical temperature profile favored freezing rain. Most days, she would attack the task with enthusiasm, finding a kind of aesthetic gratification in working out the intricacies and permutations of possibility. It was like creating a temperament, only for a much larger system than 12 tones, and perhaps that was why she found it hard to focus on it right now. It was an oblique reminder of her harpsichord, and she felt a pang of guilt and sadness that she had neglected her instrument for so long. Sitting untouched for two and a half months, it was no doubt way out of tune, and the mercurial weather of the coming spring would, as always, complicate its care. What a mess all three choirs would be even now. She resolved at least to tune it soon. Just when, though, she wouldn't promise. So much needed to be done before spring.

She shook her head and tried to focus on listing the variables involved in freezing rain and the corresponding difficulties in measuring them. But her thoughts drifted again, and she found herself fingering the accompaniment to *Peter Grimes*. It was the same aria as earlier: *In dreams I've built myself some kindlier home.* She let it run in the background of her mind as she thought of her own home, where Rob was probably cleaning up after supper, maybe making some forbidden coffee, maybe listening to Tracy bemoan her lot as a stay-at-home mom.

The sacrifices people made and then complained about. For kids. For career. For music.

I've seen in stars the life that we might share.

She recalled against her will that cold winter day in the second year of their marriage when she and Rob were in a chilly outpatient operating room. He was groggy, sitting up on the operating table, and the nurse motioned to her to help him down. She sprang toward him, glad for the chance to do something useful. She put her arm around him in gratitude, and he clung to her as she guided him behind a curtain where he could get dressed. He was so glad to sit down on that stool. He looked up at her, drool on his lips, embarrassed, needing assurance. She smiled at him—a genuine smile—and told him, yes, of course this was a good idea.

He should not have had to ask. They had both agreed. They had each other, and that would be enough.

But dreaming builds what dreaming can disown.

Morgan suddenly wondered with unreasonable alarm whether Rob was painting right now. Lately, she'd seen him working with pastels in his basement office whenever she went down there. He was always slouched over his work, as if protecting it, and he didn't look up as she passed. She didn't ask to see what he was working on, and he didn't offer to show her. She felt a pang of regret and a flash of anger almost at the same time, as if his drawing had been meant as an undeserved reproach.

She looked again toward her radar data and craved more echoes to analyze. The aria was still running through her head: *I hear those voices that will not be drowned, calling.*

Morgan slammed her fist down on her mousepad.

Susan was working at the long-range station, several paces away. She looked up at Morgan, forehead furrowed. "What now?" she asked.

"I don't know!" Morgan took her head between her hands and shook it hard. When she looked at Susan's sympathetic face, she asked, "What do you do when Bart's unhappy and unreasonable at the same time?"

Susan's eyebrows went up in surprise, but she smiled, happy to be able to give solicited advice for a change. "I stay away."

"But he's unhappy. Don't you feel like you ought to do something?"

"If he's unreasonable, I can't help him. Can't get close to someone who's running away. I tell you what, it'll only tire you out and not do one bit of good."

"Rob isn't running away though. I feel like he wants me to help, but I can't. He's just so unreasonable."

"Oh, that's different. He thinks he's being reasonable."

Morgan thought a moment. "Yeah. He does. Can't understand why I object." She turned back to her computer, shaking her head.

"Object to what?"

"A couple of weeks ago, he took out my dad's oils and started painting in our dining room."

"And you object because?"

"They're my dad's paints! And he was using them up."

"Well that's easy!" Susan was delighted to have a solution. "Buy him his own set!"

"No, it was like he wanted to use Dad's. And he got all hurt and offended when I asked him to stop." She felt the lie catch in her throat, and she realized how deep her shame was, how much she was fighting against acknowledging it. Her face became very hot, and she stared at the county lines on her computer screen as if they could anchor her thoughts. "I *was* really angry. And he said some pretty mean things. Then he smiled. Like he'd figured something out." She looked back at Susan. "But he didn't. He didn't! It hasn't been the same between us since."

Susan pursed her lips. "He and your dad got along or not?"

"They were good friends. Dad thought Rob was a pretty good artist with charcoal and pastels, and over the past couple of years, he'd been trying to get Rob to paint." Morgan grabbed a tissue and blew her nose. "And that's his excuse."

"Then Rob's just trying to work through his grief."

"But they're my dad's paints!" Morgan was crying so much she couldn't understand her own words. "They just mean a lot to me."

Susan stood next to Morgan, her hand on Morgan's shoulder. "I guess they mean a lot to Rob too."

"But he's *my* father."

"Sh sh sh, it's OK." Susan rubbed her hand on Morgan's back. "You miss your dad a lot. It's OK."

"Yeah. All the time. I mean, it's not like I talked to him all the time, but I always talked to him in my head—you know, telling him what I'm working on. Especially the music." She wiped the tears out of her eyes and grabbed another Kleenex. "I'd talk to him about weather too sometimes. But he's hopelessly unscientific!"

Susan smiled and nodded her head. She squeezed Morgan's shoulder.

"I'd have to put it into musical terms, or color, or rhythm, and that was kind of fun." She looked down at her hands and fingered a mordent on the edge of the computer table. She felt another pang. Sadness. Hopelessness. "Yeah. I really miss him." And she began to cry all over again.

After a few moments, Susan said, "Ever talk to Rob about that kind of stuff?"

"Oh sure—weather, all the time. Even in the last few weeks. We can always talk about weather. Used to be music too. He's not a musician like Dad, but he has a good ear. I've often been surprised at how much he hears. But not lately. We don't talk about music anymore."

"Painting?"

Morgan frowned. "No. I mean, we used to."

"But not anymore."

"Right. And we'd talk more about other kinds of art than about painting. Rob talked to Dad about painting."

She didn't want to talk about this anymore. Jack would be coming in soon, and she couldn't stand for an intern to see her so broken up. "Thanks, Susan. I'm sorry to fall apart like this."

"Don't mention it. I wish I could help more."

"It's OK." She dried her eyes and resolved not to cry anymore. "I'm OK now."

Ford

Of course I knew Morgan's father was Jon Tallis. I'd heard of him before I'd even met her. She looks a little like the pictures I've seen of him. Dark blond, fair skin, small and wiry, sharp nose and sharp chin. Eyes a bit too large. You wouldn't call Morgan beautiful, but she's attractive in an insidious Ice Queen sort of way.

I'm not being mean. It's just an observation. There's something about Morgan, a detachment, that entices at the same time as it makes you hopeless. She knows it too. It's deliberate.

Which was why it was so disturbing when I came upon her at the university back in early December, playing the Steinway in the old recital hall. She was so vulnerable, like all her sharp winter edges had melted into a cruel soggy spring. I don't like seeing Morgan vulnerable. It upsets my frame of reference.

I was heading past the stage door of the recital hall after a lesson with a student when I heard Bach and stopped. Three-part invention number 11. Lovely. Played firmly, intelligently, but so sorrowfully it transcended all rationality. After only a few phrases, I knew it was Morgan. No one else around here plays Bach like that.

Eleven has few ornaments—a trill after the initial exposition and a couple of mordents later on the first page, but after that, it's like Bach didn't have the heart to go on embellishing grief. It's the push and pull of dissonance and consonance, over and over, as if he wanted to extricate himself from the pain but still wanted to hang on to something he loved.

In an unequal temperament, g minor was well suited to expressions of love and grief, and this was both. Yeah, Bach knew what he was doing. Morgan did too. So why was she playing it on the piano when a harpsichord would have made the color of the tonality evident? It was odd.

I looked through the small window in one of the double doors and saw her back. Her shoulders were shaking as if she were laughing or crying, but it didn't seem to disrupt her hands at all. Her small, agile fingers moved with confidence and loving precision over and into the keys. To say each movement was a caress would be an unconscionable simplification.

It's one of the many things I admire about Morgan, her ability to alter her keyboard technique from piano to harpsichord and back. In her hands, this piece on piano had such expressive dynamics and such smooth phrasing that you could almost believe it was sung, and then she could turn around and play it on harpsichord using an entirely different pattern of fingering, articulation, and timing that pulled every last ounce of beauty from the space between the intervals.

But that day, the harpsichord was on the other side of the building, and it was Morgan playing the piano alone, shaking. I waited for a couple of students to take their conversation past me before I opened the leather-covered door and stepped onto the stage. I didn't want her to hear me. I just wanted to be there with no explanation, like an answer to a prayer.

And she didn't hear me. She finished the last few bars, then slumped over the keys and sobbed.

"Morgan?"

She looked back at me, hopeful. Her face was haggard, cheeks hollowed out, eyes tired and dark. Then she turned away, embarrassed, tears all over her face.

I came over to the narrow bench and tapped her on the arm a couple of times, and she made room for me. She continued to look down at the keys though.

"That was beautiful," I said, "as usual. More than usual. Number 11?"

"I played that at the state solo and ensemble competition in 11th grade," she said, looking down at her hands resting on the keys. Then she turned them over like she didn't recognize them, and I could see just the ends of the two old scars on her left wrist, smooth and white.

"You had to play a three-part invention at the state festival." She looked at me. "It's such a sad piece."

I nodded. After a moment, I said, "I don't think I've ever heard it played that mournfully."

"When Mom died—I was 12—that's when I learned this for the first time. Dad—" A sob caught in her throat. "Dad … he would play it sometimes … so sad." I had a hard time understanding everything she said. "And then he asked me to play … while he was painting … sometimes. So I learned it … so much pain back then."

"I thought it was you. But I wondered why you were playing Bach on a piano."

She exhaled a puff of air. It could have been a laugh or a sob. She said nothing for a long time. When she spoke, it sounded like she was talking to someone else. "I was playing harpsichord last week. The kids next door were playing in the snow. I could hear them through the closed window." A fresh tear rolled down her cheek.

I put my hand on her shoulder. Her bones felt delicate, frail. It was a foreign feeling. I realized that I'd never rested my hand on her shoulder before. Strange, given all the years I've known her. It made me very uncomfortable, like I would crush her if I made a false move.

She said, "The phone rang." Then she laid her head down on the piano and cried.

After a few minutes, I asked, "Someone died, didn't they?"

She nodded, head still down, tears dripping on the keys. "My dad."

Of course, there's nothing to say. I just pressed her shoulder a little.

After a while, I began to feel stupid, so I started talking. My father always told me it was the last thing a person should do when they felt stupid, but it seems to serve me just as well as silence. I talked about Jon Tallis.

"I liked your dad's work. Those big abstract things."

She sat up and nodded.

"He was a musician?"

"He liked to play piano. We had a Steinway baby grand in the room next to his studio, and he'd come in and play Bach when he wanted to take a break from painting. I first learned inventions from the Schirmer edition he grew up with. He had a beat-up copy of Book 1 of *The Well-Tempered Clavier* too. He loved Bach."

I remembered a painting of his that I saw once. It was on a ground of high-gloss black paint that looked almost like enamel, like a Steinway. But you could see the curve, feel the curve in the piano's side, even though the canvas was flat. I wondered a long time how he did that. There were reflections of color and light—hints of jewel tones that in a few places resolved themselves into lines of brilliant colors—and there was a quality of time to it. You expected the reflections to shift when you walked past. It was like music too, rhythmic. Not a Bach invention though. It was more like background music, like a quiet tone poem played in a bar. It was so lovely that it couldn't help but intrude on idle conversation, turn it into something deeper than business or even pleasure.

I said, "There was a painting of his I saw once called *Piano Music*."

She looked at me, surprised. "You saw that? It was sold to a private collector 12, 13 years ago. It hung in our music room at home when I was growing up." She tilted her head, as if looking at it in her mind. "But we took it down." She shrugged. "After I went to college." She shrugged again, and I took my hand off her shoulder. "And then it was just in storage, so when he had a show in Stuttgart a few years later, he decided to sell it."

"That's where I saw it. It was like reflections in the curve of a grand piano—"

"It was me." She was smiling now. "I used to stand beside the piano and make faces in it when I was five or six. Dad used to squat down next to me and make them too. And then one day he wrapped me up in a bunch of colored scarves, and I danced and jumped around next to the piano while he made sketches with pastels."

"He should've called it *Morgan* then."

"Oh, no. That's not nearly as good a title as *Piano Music*." She looked down again and lost her smile. She cried. "I miss him. God, I miss him."

She sat up after a while and wiped the tears off her face. I gave her the only handkerchief I had, the one from my breast pocket. A nice silk one, indigo paisleys on an ivory background. She stopped crying and raised an eyebrow at me as if to say, I'm supposed to use that? But she took it anyway, wiped her hands and the keyboard with it, and then blew her nose. She handed it back to me folded, dry sides out. She had a slight smirk on her face. Just a whisper, but I saw it.

She got up from the bench and picked up her portfolio. She hadn't been using a score. "Thanks, Ford," she said. "Thanks for remembering him."

"I almost bought that painting," I said. "*Piano Music.*"

She laughed! "What? Anticipating a recording contract that never materialized?"

That was too close to the mark, and she should've known better. Not all of us are as content as she is to be on the second tier.

"Something like that."

If I had known Morgan at the time I saw her father's painting, I probably would have bought it. It would have been well worth that $8,500 I didn't have and never would have.

Morgan left without saying anything else. I think she should have apologized.

Five

Picking her way between ice patches, Morgan walked through the Wolverton Civic Center parking lot on a cold, bright Saturday morning in early March. When she looked up from the pavement to orient herself toward the theatre lobby, she was surprised to see Isabel's daughter, Emilia, sitting on the steps outside, a scowl crumpling her face. Morgan had seen her a few times since that rehearsal with Isabel that had turned sour but only *after* a session with Isabel. Emilia would be waiting outside the studio with her gym bag slung over her shoulder, huffing with impatience, her hands deep in the pockets of her jeans. But she always smiled on seeing Morgan, saying "Hi!" with an open-ended inflection, as if hoping for a conversation. That was probably meant to annoy her mother. Emilia said nothing to Isabel if she could get away with it.

If the girl had to wait, Morgan wondered, why didn't she at least go into the lobby out of the 20-degree cold. The answer then presented itself: Emilia raised a cigarette to her lips.

Morgan felt an overwhelming sense of disappointment, even more than the usual sadness she felt when she saw kids sneaking a smoke in the city park. She stopped for a moment and blinked in the bright sunlight. Emilia noticed her and smiled in greeting.

"Hey, Emilia," Morgan called and resumed her careful amble over the ice. "I thought you'd be at your gymnastics lessons." Emilia's gym bag sat next to her on the step.

"So did I. The teacher's sick today." Emilia didn't make any attempt to hide her cigarette, but she did snuff it out in a patch of ice. She closed her hand around the butt, which was pretty long and probably still smokeable. "You'd think the teacher could send us all a text message or something."

"Well, there's no reason to sit out in the cold, especially with no hat or gloves." She paused several steps below Emilia when she was at her eye level. "I can let you into a studio if you want. You play piano?"

Emilia twisted her face in distaste. "I'm not a musician."

"What a shame. But I guess we can't all be insecure egomaniacs."

Emilia laughed and put her partially smoked cigarette in her gym bag. "You won't tell my mom, will you?"

"About your smoking? Why not?"

"Because she'd be mad."

"But I thought that was the whole point."

"Huh?"

"You smoke to make your opera-singer mom mad."

"No," Emilia said, as if that were the stupidest idea in the world. "I smoke because it's fun."

"Yeah, you look like you're having a great time freezing your butt off out here."

Emilia looked confused for a moment and then frowned. "Go ahead then. Tell her."

"It's not any of my business. Besides, I wouldn't have to tell her. She'll smell it on you for herself." Morgan grinned. "Maybe you should stay out here and air out a bit."

Emilia's frown smoothed out, and she looked at Morgan sidelong. "Maybe I will."

There was an awkward silence in which Morgan felt the gulf between their ages. "I'm 36," she said. "You're 13, aren't you?"

"Yeah," Emilia said, looking at her with suspicion.

"My mom started smoking when she was 13."

"Is this going to be a lecture on how your mother died of lung cancer when she was 60?"

"No." Morgan looked up at the sky and squinted. It was bright and empty except for a single contrail in the west. "She died of breast cancer when she was 34."

Emilia rolled her dark brown eyes and dug her cigarette out of her gym bag again and lit up in defiance. "Well," she said, "I don't smoke that much."

"Yeah. I can see that." Morgan checked her watch and saw that she had five minutes before she was supposed to meet Isabel. She looked at the sky again and wondered what to say. The contrail was high up, at the edge of the troposphere, turning to ice before it sublimated into invisibility.

"What are you looking at?" Emilia asked.

"Just that contrail. The jet went by probably five minutes ago. It's dry up there today, otherwise it'd turn into a cirrus cloud."

"You sound like a science teacher."

"I suppose I am in a way. I'm a scientist who trains other scientists."

Emilia laughed as if Morgan had told a mildly funny joke. "I thought you were a musician."

"I'm that too. But I spend more time as a meteorologist."

"Like on the Weather Channel?"

"Something like that, but I'm not on TV. I work for the National Weather Service behind the scenes."

"So do you chase storms?"

"Not deliberately. I've been out with storm chasers, mostly when I was in college, but I like plain old forecasting better. It's a lot more practical."

"You use radar or what?"

"Radar's where we get a lot of the data we analyze. Along with different kinds of satellite photography." Morgan felt Emilia looking at her. "I'll show you around the office sometime." Then she looked at Emilia's cigarette. "I'm afraid there's no smoking though."

"Like I'd think there was?" She sounded annoyed and looked away, but then she smiled and blew smoke into the air. "My mom wouldn't like it. She wants me to take piano lessons."

"It's not like you couldn't do both."

"No, I mean she'd make me take piano lessons before I could go. That's the way she is. I can't do anything I want until I do what she wants."

"So what'd you have to do to take gymnastics lessons? Or is that something you're doing to get to something else?"

"It was her idea." Emilia chuckled. "But I wanted to take them. So all I had to do was act like I didn't." She looked at Morgan, her expression becoming serious. "Don't tell her that."

Morgan laughed. "OK. But tell me this. Is it music you don't like or just musicians?"

Emilia shrugged. "Maybe both. Music's OK, I guess. I just don't want to be a musician."

"Why's that?"

"I don't know. Just don't." Emilia looked at her cigarette, as if gauging how many drags were left. Then she looked at Morgan, inspired. "Do you give piano lessons?"

A voice pierced the cold air behind them. "Emilia! What the hell is that cigarette doing in your hand?"

Isabel was upon them in two seconds. She reached down, plucked the cigarette from her daughter's hand, threw it on the ground, and stomped on it. Then she pulled Emilia to her feet and grabbed her shoulders. "How can you do this? Don't you know what it does to your lungs and your voice?"

"I'm not a *singer*, so what do I care?"

"You're not old enough to know what you want."

"Lungs come in handy for a lot of other things," Morgan put in.

Isabel glowered at Morgan. "You shut up! You ought to be ashamed of yourself—giving a kid a cigarette."

"You think I carry cigarettes around? As I just told Emilia, my mom died of cancer in her 30s!"

"So you stand here talking to her, as if it's…." Unable to find words, Isabel turned her attention back to Emilia, who looked as unmoved and defiant as ever. Isabel let go of one shoulder and slapped her face. Emilia's head snapped to one side, and Morgan gasped and rushed up the steps toward her. Emilia looked back at her mother, eyes narrowed and mouth pursed in hatred. Isabel raised her hand to strike again, and Morgan grabbed her shoulder.

Isabel wheeled around and slapped Morgan. The blow was sharp, and the force of it made her teeter on the steps. She had to twist her torso hard to regain her balance. She felt adrenaline and fear surging through her. Once she regained her stability, she saw that Isabel was breathing hard and looked ready to fight. Morgan was breathing just as hard, and her cheek was stinging.

Emilia stood behind Isabel, wide-eyed. "Mom!" she said, almost in a whisper. "You can't *do* that!"

Isabel's glare faltered, and her glance flitted back to Emilia and forward again to Morgan. There were tears in her eyes, and Morgan felt her frustration as if it had come off her in a wave. Isabel frowned, then crossed her arms and looked down at the ground. "I apologize." Her voice was soft but cold.

Before Morgan could find her voice to respond, Isabel grabbed Emilia's arm and jerked her toward the lobby door. Emilia's gym bag was still on the ground.

Morgan watched them go indoors, aware of an inner chill that was at least as cold as the air. She hoped Emilia was OK, and she felt helpless and angry. And ashamed.

*   *   *

It had been a very different kind of March day 10 years before when Morgan was finishing up her master's in meteorology and playing harpsichord for the Early Music Society. It was a balmy 65 degrees as she hurried to the university's Music Building, almost late for the Monteverdi concert rehearsal. She'd lost track of time at the meteorology department's computer lab, playing with a new simulation that had just come online. By the time she resurfaced from exploring all the long-term permutations of the observation data, she was running a half-hour behind. Even in her haste, however, she observed that almost 40 percent of the students on campus were wearing shorts and T-shirts. She smiled and shook her head at wishful thinking.

A huge mass of arctic air was pinned in place over the Northwest Territories by the northern jet stream, not unusual for this time of year. All it would take was a dip in the jet stream, a strong crack of the whip that rolled onto the continent from the Pacific, for that polar mass to creep southward. And if conditions were right for a low pressure system to form along the resulting cold front—and a combination of computer models indicated such an event was likely—they would be in for a major winter storm within a week. If the low pressure system intensified enough to wheel the cold front through the Midwest, with this huge swath of humid air blanketing the area, there was plenty of moisture for a significant snowfall. Then all these people trying so hard to believe in an early spring would have to get their winter coats out of storage.

Morgan expected the harpsichord to be passably in tune. The air pressure had remained steady, and though the temperature had climbed, the effects would have been counteracted by a slight drop in humidity. She did want to check that bent F-sharp pin though. As she walked into the rehearsal hall, she spotted the director, deep in conversation with the singers. Probably three or four minutes before rehearsal would start. Setting her score down on the bench, she sounded the octave in question with her left hand. Not bad was her first impression, and she closed her eyes and concentrated on the pitch, listening for beats—

The force of the blow from behind rammed Morgan's hips into the harpsichord.

"Morgan! Look! I got to wear shorts today!" Callie's voice was muffled by the pain Morgan felt in her right hand, which was wedged between her body and the lower manual. The pain traveled up her arm and, unbidden, bubbled out of her throat in a stifled howl.

"It wasn't my fault!" Callie protested in a faint and frightened voice. "I didn't do anything!"

Morgan looked at her hand and tried to move her fingers. When she couldn't, she started to shake her hand desperately, terrified that it was paralyzed by something more than pain. All her knuckles felt hyper-extended, and a red line cut across the back of her first through third fingers. It started to drip. There was a red smudge on three adjoining keys on the lower manual.

"Callie," Morgan said through her teeth, "you're too big to hurl yourself around like that."

Callie didn't seem to be there. Morgan saw her trying to run away through a crowd of people. Morgan sank into the harpsichord's bench and laid her head on the nameboard. The incoherent murmuring all around her began to coalesce: "Morgan? Are you all right?" "What happened?" "Should we take her to the hospital?" "Let's get her over to the clinic."

"No, no, no," she whispered. When she closed her eyes, the voices faded.

*   *   *

The cheek Isabel had slapped no longer hurt, but Morgan kept checking it as the morning progressed as if expecting to find a wound. The only thing she noticed was that it felt warm. It made the cold still air around her seem soothing.

Since she now had some time before that afternoon's *Peter Grimes* rehearsal, she picked up a few things at the grocery store and headed home. As she drove up to the house, she noticed Tracy leaning into the minivan parked next door. Morgan assumed she was putting her son, Mac, in a car seat. Or trying to get him out. Tracy's four-year-old daughter, Katie, began jumping up and down next to her mother, demanding attention. Their driveway was icy in spots, like everyone's. Morgan started across the narrow snowfield between their driveways with the intention of preventing the accident that was in the making, but Katie slipped and went down before she got there, hitting Tracy with her boot and knocking her off-balance. Tracy went down and caught Katie's shoulder as she tried to break her fall, forcing it into the ice. Katie wailed, of course, and Tracy gave a wretched cry, followed up with a whispered "Damn!"

Tears streamed down Tracy's cheeks, and it was apparent that she had been crying even before Katie slipped. Her jeans had a small tear in the knee where she hit the pavement, and Morgan could see a bit of blood underneath the torn denim. Katie's wails were loud, piercing, and astonishing in duration. The kid had the right stuff to become an opera singer, Morgan thought as she lifted Katie off the pavement. Tracy, sitting down on the ice with her knees sprawled apart, pulled Katie to her, saying, "Oh, Katie, honey, I'm so sorry. Are you OK, sweetie? Are you OK?" Katie just kept howling.

Morgan said, "Are you OK, Tracy?" but she couldn't get Tracy's attention. She took off Katie's hat as Tracy hugged the girl tightly (probably making any bruises worse, Morgan thought) and checked for blood and abrasions. She found a small lump forming on the back of Katie's head, tender, to judge by Katie's reaction.

Morgan put her hand on Tracy's shoulder. "She's got a bump on the back of her head, but I'm sure she'll be fine." She tried to make her voice soothing, but that was hard when she had to climb to a higher decibel level than Katie's. "Why don't we get some ice on it. And bandage up your knee, while we're at it."

Tracy seemed to become conscious of Morgan somewhere in the

middle of this, and she burst out into frustrated sobs. "I can't get Mac out of the car seat."

"How about I try to take care of that, and you can take Katie inside. She really ought to have some ice on that bruise before it gets too big."

Tracy nodded and said, "Thanks so much, Morgan. That's real nice of you." Getting up from the pavement was awkward for her, with Katie in her arms. "I'm just about at the end of my rope."

Morgan felt irritated with her, just when she knew she should have felt sympathy. She took a deep breath and heaved a sigh, and the cold air purged some of the warm anger that was rising inside her. She turned to Mac in the backseat, who was also wailing.

"Hey, buddy, what's the matter?" Morgan said in a breathy soprano. "You didn't slip on the ice—no you didn't—so what are you crying about, huh?" Mac was about 18 months old, and Morgan's words had no discernible effect on him. He had wriggled free of his wool hat, and his ears were very red—whether from the cold or the crying, it was impossible to tell. "Aw, I'll bet it's the noise," she said, as if making conversation. "Too much screaming and crying, huh? Can't beat 'em, so join 'em." She saw that the two pieces of the car seat's plastic clasp had been inserted incorrectly—one of the prongs was outside the slot and the two pieces had been jammed together and were now stuck fast. She felt a stab of indignant shock. How could Tracy not have noticed her baby wasn't secured properly? At the end of her rope indeed. In an accident, the clasp could have broken and Mac gone flying. Did she want him to die?

Morgan removed her leather glove and put her hand on Mac's head as if blessing him. "Poor Mac. You're home safe. You're OK." He continued to cry, but his wails were less forceful after a few seconds. But when she took her hand away and he could see her clearly, he started crying even harder than before. "I know, I know," she said. "You want your mommy."

Morgan worked at the stuck clasp. She managed to free it with some gentle nudging in three different directions. She lifted Mac out, who was still crying and now fighting too, and she retrieved his hat from the middle of the back seat with some difficulty. On the way into the house, she rocked him back and forth in the manner she'd seen mothers do, though his crying began to jangle her nerves.

Morgan walked onto the railless concrete porch and stepped through the front door into the living room, which would have felt open and airy if it wasn't filled with the toys and clutter of a house with a young family. With Mac's crying in her ears and Katie's wailing from the kitchen, the sense of chaos was palpable. It was warm and humid. They had to have a humidifier running, she thought, and she wondered if they kept it clean enough. The heavy air didn't feel healthy. Mac interrupted his crying to give out a little cough, much as Morgan felt like doing herself. But his bawling settled down to a whimper as he breathed familiar air in familiar surroundings. She realized that the house was welcoming in its own chaotic way, and it felt very much alive to her. It made a lump form in her throat.

She remembered being in her mom's kitchen, one time in particular. Bach had been playing on a small radio with the incongruous accompaniment of the piercing whistle of the tea kettle. The kettle had been whistling for two or three minutes, but Morgan wasn't allowed to do anything with the stove, so she couldn't turn down the flame, even though she knew how and had long been big enough to reach the controls. She was wearing pajamas and knelt on the window seat in the breakfast nook. She wiped one pane of the window with her hand, trying to see outside past the wet streaks of cold condensation. The backyard looked weird, and she was still a little confused about why she wasn't going to school. It was the first snow day of her six-year-old life.

There were huge drifts of white brilliance in the backyard, and she thought she couldn't be seeing things right through the streaky window. The seats of the swing set weren't there. The chains lost themselves in the whiteness. And some of the trees looked short, like if they'd been people, they wouldn't have had legs.

Beyond the Bach and the tea kettle, Morgan heard the piano, several rooms away. Dad had started playing some kind of jolly piece. Mom hurried in to take the kettle off the flame before it boiled dry, and the comforting smell of Mom's cigarette floated in through the saturated air. Mom took a dish towel and cleared a spot off the window so she could see out. She laughed and said with a lilt of singsong, "Looks like we'll be playing in the snow today!" Mom playing! That made Morgan laugh.

In her sudden reminiscence, Morgan had stopped moving, and Mac was loud in his complaint, pulling her back to the present. She bounced him up and down, and he fussed less.

From the kitchen, she heard Tracy pleading with Katie. "No, no, honey, Mommy's not mad at you." She was putting ice in a bag. "It was just an accident. Not your fault." Katie's crying was still loud, though her phrases weren't as long as they had been outside.

Tracy wrapped the ice bag in a towel and put it on the back of Katie's head. Katie screamed and threw the ice bag on the floor. Tracy took a deep breath and collapsed in a chair, defeated. She ran her hand through her short brown hair and pulled at the ends.

"Here," Morgan said, holding Mac out as she came into the kitchen, "Mac wants his mommy, I think." Tracy gave Mac a hug, and he quieted down right away. She set him on her injured knee. Morgan retrieved the ice bag.

"Hey, Katie," Morgan said, kneeling down in front of the girl, who was sitting on the floor with her legs bent in an array of acute angles. Katie stopped crying for a moment at the novelty of a relative stranger addressing her by name. Her eyes were very large and dark. "Got a bump on your head, huh?" The girl nodded. "Does it hurt?" She nodded again. "This'll make it feel better." She shook her head with ferocity and started crying. Morgan looked up at Tracy and smiled. "She knows her mind, doesn't she?"

Tracy twitched her mouth and bounced Mac a little on her knee. Her hair was standing out from her head on one side where she had pulled at it.

"Your head will hurt even more if you don't put ice on it," Morgan said. "The ice keeps the bump from getting bigger."

"Morgan, you can't reason with children."

Morgan looked at Tracy bouncing Mac on her knee, and she seemed to be smiling, smug.

"Nothing's ever simple, is it? What should we do then?"

Tracy shrugged. "If she doesn't want the ice on her head, she doesn't want the ice on her head."

Morgan's mouth opened in disbelief. She was only four, not old enough to reason, but Tracy was letting her decide on the course of treatment for a head injury.

"Well, what do you want me to do?" Tracy seemed to be close to tears again.

Morgan turned away from her and looked at Katie. She was still whimpering and snuffling, but looking at Morgan with curiosity. Morgan picked up a child-sized sweatshirt from the floor, hot pink. "Let's do something silly, OK, Katie? Let's make a silly hat out of this shirt." She tried to tie the shirt with the ice bag inside it around Katie's head, but the girl fought her off. "OK then. I'll wear the silly hat." Katie was unimpressed and sniffed a few times. "How about Mac? Maybe he'll want the silly hat."

Katie appeared to have second thoughts, then shook her head and reached out for the shirt. She said something that might have been "Katie shirt!"

"Oh, this is Katie's shirt?" Morgan asked. "Well, that settles it. Katie gets the silly hat." She carefully put the sweatshirt around Katie's head and tied the arms over her forehead. "Well. Isn't that pretty?"

"Silly," Katie corrected her.

"Silly," Morgan said.

She didn't have time to feel proud of herself though because after five seconds Katie took the sweatshirt off her head, removed the ice bag, and hugged the hot pink to her chest. "Katie shirt," she said with great defiance.

Tracy laughed. "Too bad Rob's not here. He's real good with the kids."

Morgan felt an electric stab in the pit of her stomach.

"It's too bad you don't have any," Tracy went on. She seemed glad that Morgan was still on the floor with Katie, so she could look down her nose. "But I guess that's not your thing."

Morgan scrambled up from the floor. Her face was warm, and she needed to get outside in the cold air. "Take care," she tried to say, but she didn't seem to have room in her chest for breath. Her heart was racing as she left the house, and she didn't know why there were tears in her eyes.

*   *   *

Morgan unloaded groceries onto the kitchen counter and tried to recapture her normal breath. Why did she feel so guilty? What did she have to feel bad about? Helping a neighbor out? Being concerned that a child was hurt?

Failing to protect Emilia?

Slapping Rob?

She threw a bag of frozen peas into the freezer, and they came rolling back out and fell to the floor. The bag split, and all at once little spheres of green were all over the kitchen.

"Goddamn!" She tugged a broom out of the closet and leaned on it as sobs overtook her breathing.

When the wave of sobs had passed, she looked up over the broom handle and out the kitchen window. All that bright untouched snow. She wondered how long it had been since anyone had played there. She tried to remember whether she and Rob had ever played there.

Backyards were for kids, never more than when they were full of snow. Even Mom had needed a little kid as an excuse to play. "I haven't seen so much snow in years," she remembered Mom saying on that first snow day years ago.

"You're going to play with me?" Morgan had asked.

"Of course! You don't get to have all the fun. Besides, I'd worry you'd fall into a snowdrift and I'd never see you again."

Morgan felt a delicious sense of danger. The backyard had never been so adventurous before. At that moment, it seemed almost as exciting as walking downtown with all its cars trying to run her over, people jostling all around, and bikes whizzing by on the sidewalk. Maybe the backyard could be even more exciting because it was so close in time and space.

Morgan tugged the towel out of her mother's hand and wiped a spot of the window dry so she could see. It was terribly bright, and the hedge at the back of the yard was erased by the snow drifts—well over her head.

"After breakfast," Mom said, "we'll go out and play."

"Will Daddy come too?"

Mom laughed her deep husky laugh. "Oh, no. It's just for us sculptors."

"I'm a sculptor?"

"You can be anything you want. But if you're going to play in a three-foot snowdrift and you're only three foot four, being a sculptor's not a bad option."

"What's an option?"

"Something that you can choose to do or not."

"Why can't Daddy be a sculptor then?"

"Oh, grownups don't have as many options for what they can be."

"Why not?" It seemed to Morgan that grownups did whatever they wanted.

"Just seems to work out that way."

Mom said that a lot. Morgan knew that to keep asking questions after that would make Mom mad. But she wasn't mad now. She was smiling.

After breakfast, she and Mom pulled on their snow gear. "*Det är inte dåligt väder, bara dåliga kläder*," Mom said.

Morgan knew that was Swedish, something Grandma used to say to Mom when she was a little girl in Minnesota. "No such thing as bad weather," Morgan said to show she remembered.

"Only bad clothes," Mom finished. She grinned and tousled Morgan's hair before pulling a thick wool stocking cap over her head. Morgan laughed because that's what stocking caps required and then put a bigger stocking cap on Mom's head. Mom pulled her long blond hair behind her ears and adjusted the cap and then pulled her fur-lined boots up over her snow pants.

When they got outside, Mom fell backwards into the drift nearest the back door and laughed as she disappeared. "Mommy!" Morgan called, frightened that Mom would drown, or not be able to climb out, or something, and at the same time ashamed that she was so afraid. Mom sat up and shook the snow out of her hair, stocking cap flailing. She stood up and brushed the snow off "before it melts and gets me all uncomfortable." She bounded out of the drift and directed Morgan to where the snow was shallower. She said they would make snowwomen.

Morgan knew how to make a snowman, and she figured a snowwoman would be the same. She'd made snowmen when she was really little, and she'd seen them in neighbors' yards a long time ago. You made three big snowballs by rolling little snowballs, and you had to keep changing directions while you were rolling them, otherwise you ended up with a jelly roll rather than a ball. Then you piled the three on top of one another. Mom would come up with something really neat for the top ball to make a head with eyes and ears and nose and mouth—something that would make it a snowwoman rather than a snowman. Morgan got to work and rolled three big, perfectly round snowballs.

Proud of herself, she turned to Mom, who she thought was standing by to help her stack the snowballs on top of one another. But Mom had been busy herself. Morgan saw two legs taking shape in the snow, feet folded under, as they came into being sitting on the ground. "Look, Mommy!" Morgan called, expecting her to come over and help.

Mom smiled. "That's great, honey. We can use those." She smoothed out one of the thighs and got up, not moving over to Morgan but going to the small toolshed in the corner of the yard. She had to fight through a snowdrift to get the door open. Morgan stayed where she was because she wasn't allowed to go into the toolshed on her own, and Mom hadn't asked her to go with her. Mom came out with a big saw, smiling. "Here's what we need!" she said. Then she went right up to Morgan's largest snowball and sawed a big chunk off. Then she lifted up the rest without even asking for Morgan's help and plopped it, flat side down, atop the two folded legs. "We'll give her a nice Buddha belly," she said, in a grownup voice that Morgan knew wasn't addressed to her.

Tears warmed Morgan's eyes as Mom came back for the saw without looking at her and then proceeded to shave more pieces off another once perfect snowball. Morgan sat down in the snow and cried. She knew she was being a baby, and she tried to stop, but she couldn't. Her throat hurt too much to keep the sobs in. Her fingers felt numb in her wet mittens, and her nose was stinging from the cold. Mom came back for the next snowball, but she failed to notice Morgan. When she started to cut that one up too, it was more than Morgan could take.

"Mommy! Stop it! Just…stop it!"

Mom dropped the saw and ran over to Morgan. "What's the matter? Did you hurt yourself?"

Morgan could hardly talk, but she forced herself to say, "You're ruining it! You're ruining it!"

Mom held Morgan in her arms, bewildered and uncomprehending.

And grownup Morgan, older now than Mom had ever been, stared at the blank purity of her own backyard, and another warm sob erupted from her chest.

Rob

Morgan hasn't been sleeping well lately. It's different than it was a few months ago, right after Dad died, when she had to take sedatives that were so strong she fell into a deep silent sleep where she didn't move and barely breathed. Now, it's fitful, frustrating, tossing and turning for a few hours, then wandering the house before trying again. Sometimes I wake up when she's not there. Every time in my half sleep I listen, hoping to hear the harpsichord.

Sometimes I go upstairs looking for her and find the studio empty. I think she's left me, and my breath stops dead in my chest. I grope my way back to bed, hoping it's a bad dream but not believing until morning that it is.

Twice in the past week, when I was awake enough to notice, I saw her looking out the bedroom window at the backyard. Eyes puffy from crying. When I got up and touched her, she shrugged my hands off. I didn't know if she was angry. She just seemed distant. If she had snarled, it would've made me feel better somehow, like she'd recognized me, like there was at least a thin cable connecting the two sides of the chasm between us. All the time, I'm thinking, "What's wrong, Morgan?" But I'm too groggy for my mouth to form the words.

I go back to bed with my stomach burning, dream about wolves baying at the moon. The next morning, she's gone before I get a chance to say anything. But maybe I would have just stayed quiet anyway because I'm too afraid she won't answer.

Yes, I'm a coward. I should start this conversation, insist on it. After Dad died, I gave her space because I didn't want to hurt her more than she was already hurting. But the idea that Morgan can't take it just doesn't square with the strength of her discipline. She might seem brittle, but it's not like I'm dealing with beams made of inferior steel or some poorly mixed concrete.

Here I am trying to figure out the mechanical advantage of a conversation with Morgan when I don't even know the force amplification I'm going for. I feel her drifting away from me, but I don't want to push her away faster or further.

So maybe she'll be home when I get there, and maybe I'll ask how it got to be this way. Maybe she's as scared as I am and the anger is just covering it up. Maybe I'll tell her what happened tonight, even if she doesn't ask about this huge coffee stain on my shirt, even if she doesn't notice it.

She hasn't asked about the late hours I've been keeping at the lab. I wouldn't blame her for thinking I'm avoiding her—but I'm not. I'm avoiding Tracy.

I know I should've seen it coming. Over the years I've had a few students flirt with me, maybe angling for a better grade or maybe they were actually attracted to me—I don't know. I never found out because I was always careful never to let it go anywhere. With Tracy, though, I don't think she flirted at all. How can you flirt with two little kids in tow? She was just the neighbor stopping in for a cup of coffee.

Then a couple weeks ago, we had this one conversation about kids. I told her I sometimes wished that Morgan and I had decided differently. As soon as I said it, I knew I shouldn't have—and at the time, I was only thinking of Morgan. I mean, it felt like a kind of betrayal. I wasn't thinking about what kind of impression it might make on Tracy.

The next time I saw her, though, she sat closer to me, touched my hand a few times when we were talking. Then she was there again the next day, complaining about Stu—he's not home enough, he treats her like hired help, that kind of thing. I told her flat out I'm not the person she should talk to. Then she started crying a little, all the while inching her hand toward mine. I didn't take it, even if it seemed like the most natural thing in the world.

Then she starts putting Morgan down, saying she was real snotty to her a few days before, humiliating her in front of the kids. I know Morgan can be pretty snotty when she thinks she's been provoked, but I just don't see her trying to humiliate Tracy. Especially not around her kids. She'd be too worried about what kind of emotional scars she'd be making on such young children.

Morgan has always felt very protective of children. A little too protective. I mean, she's so protective she wouldn't have children—she's too afraid that she would be a bad parent, that *we* would be bad parents together.

It's not like she forced the decision on me. It wasn't unreasonable. It was the responsible thing to do. With both of us so wrapped up in our careers, there would never be enough time for kids. We'd either resent all the sacrifices we'd have to make, or else we wouldn't make them and our kids would suffer, maybe for their whole lives. And she was right—but what about all the couples who manage to have families and two careers? Morgan would say she didn't see too many exemplary families of that type around. And she has two careers just by herself.

She's right. But ...

When we got engaged, almost 11 years ago now, we were planning on a family—two kids, boys or girls, it didn't matter. But then—then she started noticing neglected kids. I saw them too. Everywhere, it seemed. How did any of us ever get through childhood?

She got cold feet.

I did too, I guess. I did get the vasectomy after all. I remember after the procedure, she helped me down off the table. She sat me down somewhere nearby. I thought she was worried. She bent over me looking worried. So I tried to smile, said something, I don't know what. Then she smiled and said, "Yes." Her teeth looked sharp and white, she looked so happy, I knew she was OK. "Trust me," she said, and I knew I was OK because she was with me.

I never regretted it.

Not much. At least not much before Dad died—Morgan's dad. I knew he was all the family she had, but I never knew what that meant. He was like an anchor for her. For us. Now she's drifting. We're drifting. And I find I do wish we'd made different choices, that there was someone besides the two of us, someone connecting us to the future, someone we would need to be an anchor for.

I probably wish it for a lot of reasons. And now I see Katie and Mac, and part of me wishes they were mine.

But I don't wish Tracy's life on Morgan. Or me either.

What did happen between Morgan and Tracy a couple weeks back? It may not have happened the way Tracy said, but I don't think she was making the whole thing up. In fact, I think I know what day it was. I got home only a few minutes before Morgan left for rehearsal. She was looking out the kitchen window with a broom in her hand. There were frozen peas all over the floor. It was like she was listening to something. I could see she was on edge. I wanted to put my hands on her shoulders, rub the tension out of them. But I didn't.

"Morgan? Are you OK?"

"Sure," she said, sounding surprised. Or impatient. "Just got lost for a minute, that's all." She looked tired, and she'd been crying. Her eyes were red around the rim like they get. She knew I noticed. "For crying out loud, I was just remembering playing in the snow when I was a kid." She started to sweep up the peas, which weren't exactly frozen by that time. "Hadn't thought about it in years, and probably won't for another 20."

"Oh." I looked out the window at the smooth unbroken snow of our backyard. I felt a sudden childish urge to kick up a path through it. Make my mark on the world. "We should build a snowman."

Morgan gasped and looked at me as if I'd accused her of some crime.

"We don't have to if you don't want to! Jesus, Morgan." I stepped toward her and held my hand out to her. "Would you just talk to me?"

"I have to go to rehearsal." She gave me the broom and walked past me toward the door. But she turned back. Her voice caught in her throat. "Would you clean up the peas? I dropped the bag and they went all over."

Sure, I'd clean up the peas. "But what's the matter?"

"I'm running late, that's what's the matter!" She stomped out shaking her head.

After that, she started wandering around the house at night. And not long after that, I started staying late at the lab.

To avoid Tracy.

Then tonight Tracy just shows up at the lab. No kids in tow, just a thermos. Said she missed our coffee klatches. She'd never been to the lab before—I don't think she'd even been to the campus. She was just so put out that I wasn't happier to see her after she had gone to all the trouble to get a babysitter, drive to campus, and figure out where the hell my lab was. I was on the point of saying I never asked her to go to all that trouble when I saw tears in her eyes.

So I accept a cup of coffee. Say, sure we can shoot the breeze for a little while. The coffee's laced with some kind of alcohol, but I don't say anything about that, just put the cup down on my desk like I plan to pick it up again. But I never do.

Now Tracy starts in again on how snotty Morgan is. Looking down her nose at her, finding fault with her. "She actually wrinkled her nose when she handed Mac over to me."

"Well, maybe he smelled."

"Rob! You're supposed to be on my side!"

I wondered how much of the spiked coffee she drank before she got there. "How do you figure?"

She didn't answer, just made a face like I was being a smartass.

"Really, Tracy. How do you figure? I'm married to her, and I'm supposed to side with you?"

She scowled and all of a sudden threw her coffee at me. The coffee was hot and it hit me in the chest. Behind my yelps, I heard her say something like, "You two really do belong together."

Yeah, Tracy. That's how it's supposed to work.

Six

The dew point had risen into the 30s, and thin puffs of vapor formed near Morgan's nose and mouth. Thirty-five degrees wasn't exactly balmy for mid-March, but after a deep cold snap it felt springlike.

It was a tight schedule when rehearsals started at 6 p.m. Morgan was right on time, but without a minute to spare. She was dead tired and wondered for a moment whether the harpsichord would be in tune after the change in weather, lamenting that she wouldn't have time to adjust any pitches. Then she remembered: this wasn't a continuo gig—it was *Peter Grimes*, and no matter how much the weather changed, she wouldn't be able to tune the piano.

Warm dry air rushed out with a surprised whoosh as Morgan pulled open the glass door to the lobby of the Wolverton Civic Center. She heard a great tumble of vocal exercises spilling out of the open auditorium doors. The singers were wandering on and around the half-set stage as they warmed up. As she entered the auditorium, she heard the sound of the piano underneath it all, unobtrusive bass notes, struck full but short, a good imitation of pizzicato strings. Ford loitering at the piano no doubt.

God have mercy upon me, she thought, the words coming to her mind as if in her own voice. Uneasy, she assured herself that the words must have come from the music. But when she put her mind to it, she recognized the music as the ground bass from the second act's orchestral interlude—no words to that.

She made her way down to the orchestra pit. The orchestra wouldn't join the rehearsals until the following day, so there were no other instrumentalists there, though a few singers were strewn among the disordered chairs, waiting for rehearsal to begin. Ford was indeed playing the piano. No one was paying any attention to him, and he wasn't paying attention to anyone else. *God have mercy upon me*, she thought again, and this time she heard it in Ford's clear tenor.

The opera score was on the piano, open to the interlude, a passacaglia. Suddenly, she heard in the ground bass an echo of Peter's last line in the previous scene. *God have mercy upon me!* She had never noticed it before, it was so understated, disguised as accompaniment. Clever of Britten, she thought, bringing words into the orchestral music subliminally.

This version of the interlude was scored for four hands, and soon Ford would be unable to play everything. But at the moment, he could handle both parts—he had just added a melodic line to the ground bass, which would have been a mournful viola solo in the full orchestral score. Morgan had long known Ford was a talented pianist, but something about the way he played that simple line surprised and transfixed her. Like a Grimes aria, it was plaintive but menacing with pent-up energy that might at any moment explode. She felt Ford's hands were singing, almost coaxing vibrato and dynamics into sustained notes. Of course, that had to be an aural illusion, created by nuanced movement and counter-movement. But knowing it was an illusion impressed her all the more.

The passacaglia was a Baroque form, consisting of continuous variations on a ground bass. They were usually composed in a slow triple meter, unlike Britten's interlude, which was in four quarter time. Morgan felt there was a lurching quality to the ground bass, an extra beat or two that wouldn't fit into the four beats per measure of common time. No, it was a missing beat, she concluded. An eleven-beat phrase made the natural stress of the meter fall on a different pitch each time the ground bass was repeated. It felt like a desire to be, if not free of the constraints of common time, at least something other than common. The same longing was in the viola solo that Ford imitated so well, all those ties across the bar, the slow syncopation that made it difficult to find the downbeat.

Ford gave no indication of surprise when Morgan sat down next to him on the piano bench, her hands poised to take over the upper part.

He might have been expecting her for all the change in his musical demeanor. And Morgan felt no surprise to find herself there, crowded next to Ford and ready to share the keyboard as well as the music. She turned the page as the viola solo pressed on, the longing increasing in tension even while it became softer. Ford's right hand reached in front of her for the highest notes a viola could produce. Underneath, her left hand began a soft march. Its imposition of order was both cheery and threatening in its bright insistence, while Ford's ground bass maintained its steadily unsteady rhythm, claiming independence but failing to break away.

In *Peter Grimes*, sea and storm were never far away from eye or ear or mind. Maybe Morgan had never seen the ocean herself, but she knew Britten's sea, his weather, and she knew the intricate mechanical part she played right now would never survive the waves. Yet she gloried in it as the arrogance of civilization demanded, sounding a triumphant fanfare. Then immediately she had to switch perspective and give life to opposing forces: wind and waves, quick slashes of sound beating back the unnatural precision of clockwork.

Ford played the bottom line of the beating waves, following her hands up the keyboard in perfect coordination, his right hand playing only a third away from her left, and only a whisper of a touch passed between them. It was impossible that their hands didn't become entangled, but measure after measure they didn't. Ford took over the fanfare, and as if they had agreed beforehand, he took over the pedaling too. He turned the next page, maintaining the ground bass and dropping only two beats of the upper part. As the sea raged against the fanfare, they crescendoed together until the fanfare broke up under its own tension, and everything slipped back to a soft menacing calm.

But water and air are never entirely still, and Morgan played the slow swells of the sea for a few bars, relying on Ford's sense of dynamics to create the illusion of seamless crest and trough, crescendo and decrescendo in the long slow lines. Then, as from a distance, the march began again, quiet but insistent in its mechanical rhythm, and Morgan and Ford had to play in lockstep. A bystander turned the page for them, and neither missed a beat.

The march retreated after building, not to a crisis, but to a hollow show of force, as if it understood the battle couldn't be won and so wouldn't be undertaken. The waves of the sea rolled across the keys in overlapping phrases, back and forth from Morgan to Ford to Morgan to Ford. The waves receded in slow circling eddies until only Ford's ground bass was left: *God have mercy upon me.*

Morgan's part began again with percussion and muted brass, a staccato echo that blossomed into an aria for high strings, an aria that Ford—Peter, Ford as Peter—would soon pick up as his madness began to take root. The strings Morgan heard through her fingertips were like lost spirits tethered to earth by the ground bass, the uneven, lurching bass that was always there but never solid. The spirits were carried away as she played on, dissipated by the wind, and waves of brass crashed again on the shore, breaking, washing away the shreds of spirit and will.

But not the pain. Those remnants were rekindled in something of a frantic fugue where 16th notes chased each other around the middle octaves of the keyboard. They gathered energy and volume until they became a frenzied fanfare announcing the opening of the scene.

Go! Ford's strong tenor pierced the air in a shattering cadenza, a pure open vowel cutting a tortuous path to its final destination, *there!* Morgan had to lean in front of him to get to the final notes in the low bass, and though he leaned back as he sang, her left arm and shoulder still touched him, and his voice reverberated throughout her body.

Go there! Go there!

She was ready for him to go on, ready to go there, anywhere. She would accompany Peter to his watery grave, and it wouldn't be suicide. Or was it Ford she would accompany?

The music wouldn't allow her to follow, however. The next bar was hers alone, and she would have to lead the way. She hesitated, did not immediately play the segue to the rest of the aria. Then she became aware of applause, enthusiastic but muffled behind her heartbeat. She let go of the keys and looked up at Ford, still in a state of intense concentration. Ford looked at her with equal intensity and cradled her head in his right hand and kissed her, hard. When she opened her eyes, his were open too, serious. Then he smiled, a jaunty smile. A smile for the audience, the rest of the cast. She looked around, and it suddenly felt very warm and crowded, and she became aware of Isabel standing a few yards away, her beautiful face snapped away into profile, like a Victorian cameo.

Morgan began to feel frightened as her concentration decayed into disorientation, then eased into self-consciousness. Ford was no longer sitting on the bench, and she didn't look to see where he was. She would have run away if there hadn't been so many people crowded between her and the pit exit. So instead, she fussed with her score and waited for Charles to call the rehearsal to order.

*   *   *

As Morgan pulled into her driveway just after 10:30 p.m., she wiped her mouth with the back of her leather glove. It was the third time she'd caught herself in that furtive gesture.

She wanted to tell Rob about the duet with Ford, but she was dreading it. She knew that for most of the 12 years she and Rob had been together she would have told him everything—the thrill of being in the zone, of playing flawlessly without any rehearsal, even the kiss that cemented the intimacy of the moment. She would've told Rob everything without fearing his reaction, without question. It unsettled her that she questioned it now.

On the drive home, she'd kept rehearsing the conversation in her mind, trying different tacks, and always feeling the words fall apart within a few sentences, overcome in a flood of sonic memory. *God have mercy upon me.*

Morgan was surprised that Rob's car wasn't in the garage. He was usually home by now, even when he stayed late at the lab. It dawned on her that she had no idea what his schedule was these days.

The unsettled feeling revealed itself as something more specific: she missed Rob. As nervous as she was about it, she had been counting on telling him about the duet. Now it was frustrating that he wasn't here, and she didn't know where he was or when he'd be back. And it was all the more frustrating because she knew it was her fault.

She stomped up onto the porch and turned the key in the lock with unusual force. Averting her eyes from the blank wall where *Weather Map* should have been, she went to the back of the house and down into the basement. Rob's office area was over to the right, under one of the half-windows crowded up next to the ceiling. It looked unused. The desk was clear, and there were no loose papers or sketches stuck to the filing cabinet. She opened a desk drawer and saw a box of pastels on top of several used sketch books. She wanted to open them up, see what he'd been working on, but it felt too much like she didn't have the right.

She hated the way tears stung her eyes and her nose. She turned away and found the laundry area in her line of vision. That yellow shirt Rob had rinsed out was still hanging above the sink, where she had found it dripping the night before. It seemed to her now that it held a story, begging to be told.

Why hadn't Rob just told her?

Because they hadn't talked to each other in days. They hadn't talked in days, and now she was going to tell him about the duet? Maybe it wasn't such a good idea after all. It made the story so much more significant than she wanted it to appear.

Back upstairs, she stood in front of the bay window where Rob had set up Dad's easel several weeks ago. Where she had slapped him. Some of the anger came back to her when she thought of that moment, and she balled up her fists. But then those fists came up to her forehead, and she leaned into them and sobbed. Her sense of shame was overwhelming. She had never slapped anyone before. She'd never even considered slapping Isabel on the steps of the Civic Center—she just wanted to keep her from hurting Emilia. But she was still so angry! With Rob. With herself. And so ashamed, and the shame seemed old, older than the slap.

As her sobs subsided and fists loosened, she wiped her face with open hands. She should talk to Rob. He was so good at figuring things out. She wondered where he was, wondered whether he was wondering where she was or thinking about her at all. She wondered if she had pushed him so far away that he was now out of reach.

Morgan shivered and frowned. Britten's sea swelled in her sleep-deprived mind, and she didn't know whether to root for the disaffected soul rocking on the waters, for the order of civilization, or for the chaos of wind and waves. *Go!* she heard Ford cry. *Go there! Go there!*

And do what? Go where, and do what? Death was where Peter and his poor apprentice went. It was where Dad was. Go there?

Peter Grimes was full of shit.

*　*　*

When 19-year-old Morgan had come home from the hospital after cutting her wrist at Mount Hope Conservatory, Dad had cleared all the knives out of the kitchen and everywhere else in the house. He locked up or threw away everything he could think of that could be a poison. When shirts and suits came back from the dry-cleaners, the plastic wrap had been removed so she couldn't suffocate herself with it. He panicked if she took a bath instead of a shower, and he delivered her personally to her psychiatrist's office twice a week because of course he wouldn't let her drive.

All this would have irritated her to the point of rage if she hadn't seen the painting Dad had created during the two weeks she had been in the hospital. It was large, at least six feet across. The background was black textured with shades of gray and aching with ghosts of crimson and violet, even a little green. In the foreground floated vivid red petals—that was how Morgan saw them—petals that dripped, bled into the deep dark yawning background of grief. She hadn't seen such pain in Dad's work since Mom had died. She was so ashamed. She knew then, even if she had wanted to die, she would've stayed alive just to spare him.

For two weeks after she came home, Dad had someone else teach his classes at the university while he watched over her. He sat with her down in the basement in his paint-spattered jeans, sometimes for hours on end, watching the Weather Channel. Making jokes about the mete-orologists' outfits or delivery. Making judgments about the aesthetic effect of weather maps. Making sure she didn't hang herself.

Dad thought the gray background of the satellite maps was way too dull. "They need at least two colors besides the white of the clouds." He squinted judiciously as he thought about it, his pointed chin resting on his propped-up hand. "The olive and slate they use on the other maps—what do you call them?"

"Surface maps?"

"Yeah—those are OK, although maybe it'd be better with the pastel pinks and oranges you see on the old Rand McNally world maps."

"It's been done, Dad."

"You're right," he admitted. "I won't complain about the olive. But that chartreuse they use for rain—that has got to go. A little more sub-tlety please."

"But they need high contrast. You want to be able to see frontal boundaries, don't you?"

"Do I? Why?"

"It's a weather map. That's the whole point. If you were taking a trip to see me at Mount Hope, wouldn't you want to know exactly where the snow bands were?"

"I never thought about it."

"You never thought about it? If I-94 was going to be snow-covered and slippery all the way to Grand Rapids, wouldn't you want to know if another route would be clearer?"

"There's another route?"

Morgan hit him with a throw pillow.

"OK, point taken." He grinned. "High contrast. But does it have to be as garish as chartreuse?"

"I refuse to be in the position of defending chartreuse."

"And why does it always have to be counterclockwise?" His complaint was directed at the TV. "It gets boring after a while."

"Low pressure areas. They always spin counterclockwise." She glanced sideways at him, feeling she was losing her audience to the allure of color and pattern. "High pressure areas spin clockwise."

"Well, where are they?"

"There's a big one over the Rockies right now and another in the Northeast. That's what the big H stands for."

"But there's nothing there."

"High pressure areas don't have precipitation. They don't even have clouds a lot of times."

"Then how can they spin at all?"

"It's called wind, Dad. You just can't see it on the map."

"Then how do you know it's there?" He snapped his fingers as if inspired. "That's what the map needs, a color for wind."

"That might make it a little cluttered."

"You could clear out some of those counterclockwise snow-clouds."

Morgan laughed and took a closer look at the moving radar images. "I think low-pressure areas spin clockwise in the southern hemisphere. Down under, doesn't water spin the other way down a drain?"

She looked at Dad, who was looking at her as if he saw something unexpected. Then he smiled. "You're asking me?"

*　*　*

Morgan was ready for bed and wanted to be sound asleep, but she found herself instead standing in front of the closet in her studio where she had stored Dad's smaller paintings until she was strong enough to see them again. She slid the closet door to the side, raising her gaze to the overhead shelf, where she had stowed the shoeboxes of letters and photographs she had gathered from Dad's house. She took one in each hand and eased them down to the studio floor, where she sat cross-legged, her back to the closet.

The boxes had years written on the outside, and she had taken hold of two that covered a large span of her childhood. She found the contents a jumble, which didn't surprise her. Dad had been a rummager, whose sense of order was defined in much broader terms than hers. She had often observed him skimming the contents of one or another of these boxes, delighting in stumbling over an unexpected memory on the way to the expected. Morgan, on the other hand, did not enjoy rummaging if she had a goal in mind. At the moment, her goal was to find a picture of Dad, to see with her eyes as well as her mind the reflection of the unexpected in his features.

All the pictures she recalled of Dad had some look of surprise. He was the photographer in the family, she realized as picture after picture chronicled her childish exploits or the moods of her mother. There was a picture of one of his birthdays, cake glowing with thirty-odd candles, behind which he was ducking. A raised eyebrow was about all Morgan could make out. There he was again, far away in a badly composed, over-exposed shot of a group at a department picnic. And there, there he was caught in clear technicolor surprise looking at the camera, at an opening reception for an exhibition at some gallery that Morgan couldn't identify. He looked young, alarmed, and almost smiling, in his hand a glass of wine that he looked about to drop. And Mom was next to him, looking at him. She seemed angry; she had an angry profile. Like Isabel, Morgan thought. And nothing like her. Mom's blond hair was pulled back from her head, and she held an unlit cigarette by her side. Morgan wanted to look at Dad, but her eyes kept straying to Mom, feeling a kinship that seemed like a betrayal.

She turned the picture over and set it aside in the looked-at pile she was forming, then she riffled through a patch of photos taken at her early recitals. She came upon another picture of Mom, out in the snowy yard, smiling beneath a floppy stocking cap. Young Morgan was standing a few feet away, about six years old and looking like she had just wiped tears off her face. She looked angry and miserable but resigned. In between the two figures was Mom's snow sculpture, just as Morgan remembered it, except it was smaller. Behind them the seats on the swing set were lost in a huge drift of snow.

Dad took the picture, of course, black and white, well composed. She didn't remember who told her to get into the picture, but she felt even now that she had been superfluous.

The snowwoman was only a little taller than Morgan, somewhat larger than life size. And nude, with a Buddha belly and melon breasts. Distinct nipples. She was kneeling, sitting on her heels, and her hands were upturned, each resting on a knee, as if in prayer or surrender. It was her face that arrested Morgan now, however—Morgan had forgotten the face. Maybe she had never looked at it. It was peaceful, with a faint smile, and it was almost a self-portrait of Mom. Different from Mom only in its quiet peace, neither joyful nor angry nor sad. And Morgan knew, suddenly and incontrovertibly, that the snowwoman had no children.

In the picture, Mom was beaming, a proud hand on her creation's shoulder. And Morgan, little Morgan, stood to one side facing the camera but wanting to look up at Mom, wanting Mom to look at her. Morgan remembered how it was, even though all the camera caught was her resignation. Mom was a good mother, Morgan told herself. She *was* good. She couldn't help leaving. But, if only for that one day, she regretted Morgan.

Anger caught in Morgan's throat. She wanted to hold that small child and tell her that Mom loved her. Explain that the snowwoman would melt away, but she would remain, forever loved. She wanted to explain, even if she didn't feel it.

Ford

The whole incident was a blend of the theatrical and the real—we were playing parts, but it was happening to us, ourselves. She had to feel it, that coordination, that inside-and-outside thinking-as-one alignment of purposes. We were in the zone together—all that desire, chaos, sensuality, personality—jelling into a wild precision. God! I only wish it had been in the rehearsal studio rather than in front of the whole cast.

I should have thought of it before, it's so obvious. How many times have I seduced a diva while singing with her?

But it never would have worked if I'd planned it. How many piano duets do I know anyway? Besides, she came to *me*. I didn't even know she was there until she sat down next to me. It was just a serendipitous conjunction of opportunity and desire. The kiss wasn't planned either. It was simply the only thing to do.

Something changed when I kissed Morgan. That's melodramatic but true. I've been thinking about her ever since. And if I think about *that* too much, it will scare me speechless.

After the kiss, Isabel said to me, "You know it's over, Ford." I just nodded. Then she looked at Morgan sitting at the piano, waiting for rehearsal to start. She frowned, pinching her lovely eyebrows together in an ugly crease. She looked like she wanted to spit. But instead she said, "She looks scared, don't you think?"

Morgan did look scared. Like she was in a bad dream and desperate to wake up.

It must be pretty difficult for her. She has such a strong sense of propriety after all. Even though she seems unhappy with Rob lately, I think she still loves him. Hardly a pleasant thought, but it would be just like her.

I don't really mind that Isabel broke it off. It was never supposed to last, anyway. It's just unfortunate for the show. It would've been easier to feel tender toward each other on stage if we were still sleeping together off. But Isabel's a pretty good actress. The effect was minimal at last night's rehearsal, except her singing got darker—angry—on the disappointment. Charles mentioned it when he gave us our notes after the run-through, which of course made her angrier. She shot Morgan a fiery look.

I don't think Morgan took any notice of it though. She was clutching her score, worn out, concentrating on the door like she was still waiting to escape that bad dream.

The bad dream wasn't the kiss though, I'm sure of that. It was just the public venue, and that's an easy obstacle to remove.

Seven

The coffee pot was an essential piece of equipment at the National Weather Service. Sleep deprivation was passed around the operations area each month as the shifts rotated in and out of keeping with various forecasters' circadian rhythms. Sleep deprivation was no longer expected of Morgan, however, since she had become the science and operations officer and worked regular days. Still, it had to be pretty serious before Terence would mention it.

"I'm not saying there's anything wrong with your work," Terence said. "Yet. I'm saying you look like hell and you're headed for a sick bender, so take the day off tomorrow and get some sleep. And give the music a rest—that show has to be wrapping up soon, I hope?"

Morgan nodded and noticed a muscle spasm in her neck. She rubbed it. "It's opening next week, so my part's done. They're working with orchestra from here on out."

"Glad to hear it. You look like hell, Morgan."

"Thanks. You said that already."

"Bears repeating." He turned on his heel and strode back to his office. He stopped at his door and looked back, frowning like he was considering saying something. But he just gave his head a terse shake and said, "Get some sleep."

Morgan couldn't remember the last time she'd had a full night's sleep. And yet that night, she still felt compelled to wander the house. She tried to concentrate, to remember Dad without feeling pain, but her memories always circled back to children playing in the snow.

At last she went to bed and slept a broken sleep, startled again and again by an insistent and unwelcome telephone. The sound disappeared when she opened her eyes, and she was grateful it was so easy to take care of.

Sometime the next morning, it seemed like the phone was ringing again. When she opened her eyes, she knew it was late, too late to still be asleep. Rob was sitting next to her on the edge of the bed, ready to leave for the day. She blinked a few times. He smiled. It clashed with the worry lines in his forehead.

"Day off?" he asked. His voice was tentative.

"Yeah." She tried to stretch her neck. Rob didn't get up. "Terence said I looked like hell. Get some sleep, he said."

"Sounds like good advice." Rob pushed a lock of hair off her forehead. It was such a simple and comforting thing to do. She tried to smile, but it felt like gravity pulled her lips in the wrong direction.

It seemed like he wanted to say something as much as she did. He looked into her eyes and she wondered what he saw there. His smile faded, and he gave a little shrug. She closed her eyes to hide whatever it was.

"Sweet dreams," he said and kissed her on the forehead.

*   *   *

There was something comforting about handling a machine. The nature of the situation was almost always evident: understand the laws of thermodynamics, the dangers and uses of friction, the chemistry of combustion, and it was possible to handle any problems that might arise. The inexplicable could be explained, the right decision implicit in the conditions. Incorrect decisions were measurable. And if something went wrong, there would be a solution. Or at a least a clear reason for scrapping the heap.

When she couldn't get back to sleep after Rob left, Morgan sought out machines. She replaced the air filter on the furnace and cleaned the humidifier. She checked the transfer switch to the backup generator. She tossed a load of laundry into the washing machine and listened to its rhythmic churning for a few minutes, staring at Rob's yellow shirt still hanging over the sink. She sniffed at it, but it hadn't grown any more scent since Tuesday night. As usual, Rob had done a thorough job.

What had been on the shirt? And why did she care? Why was she so sure Rob was daring her to notice it? It could have been anything—a soil sample, some chemical from his lab. Paint from one of Dad's tubes (she'd counted them, though, hadn't she?). Cigar ash? Lipstick, perfume?

She was straying too far from the world of machines. She pulled the shirt down from its hanger and tossed it in with the rest of the roiling laundry, where it was soon buried in suds. It made her feel better but not good.

Back upstairs, she wandered into the bedroom and looked out the window at the backyard full of half-melted snow. It was cloudy, but the brightness was still painful, and she turned away from it. She settled her eyes on the pastel drawing that she had had matted and framed a couple years before. It was one of Rob's, and she thought he would put it up in his office on campus, but he wanted it up in their bedroom instead. It was a lovely little drawing. She always thought of it as a skewed view of ripples on the surface of water, from underneath the surface, which was a bit unsettling if she thought too much about it. It was dusky, and it really did look wet. That was what Morgan liked about it—the illusion. Rob had transformed the state of matter—he'd made solid pastels liquid or appear liquid. She found herself looking forward to seeing what he could do in oils, once he felt ready to take them up.

Then she remembered that he had indeed taken them up. And she had slapped him for it.

It wasn't Rob she didn't understand. She didn't understand herself. And that was one puzzle she never enjoyed trying to solve, particularly when she wasn't thinking straight to begin with.

A few minutes later, she was gazing at the CD collection above the stereo in the living room. The dust layer was visible. Nothing appealed to her. Baroque would remind her of Dad. Or Ford. Twentieth century would remind her of Rob and late nights in her studio. Romantic music would remind her of Leo Neville and her failure as a pianist. What was left? Classical maybe?

The decision became too taxing, and she ended up just pressing the power switch on the stereo and setting the controls to tuner. In a few seconds, the room filled with "Sleepers, Awake!" She laughed.

An image came to mind: a fogged up window and a small hand—her hand—wiping at the cold moisture so that she could see the brilliant white beyond. She smelled the smoke from Mom's cigarette, heard the insistent whistling of the tea kettle. "Sleepers, Awake!" behind it all.

"What's that on the radio?" she asked as Mom breezed into the kitchen.

"Bach's greatest hits." Mom shrugged and smiled. Grownup Morgan smiled at the memory—it was just like Mom. And "Sleepers, Awake!" wasn't such a good title anyway. If anything, the music was soothing, more like a lullaby. Morgan, sitting on the sofa in front of the empty fireplace, wondered if sleeping wasn't a better way of waking up after all.

She heard Mom laughing in the snow as she sawed through a big snowball. Morgan wanted to see what she was laughing at, but she couldn't turn her head. Ford was kissing her, and turning away would've been rude. The kiss lasted a long time, and Morgan wondered if Ford's lips would get tired, kissing so hard for so long. Were her lips tired? She was kissing him back. They must be. Kids were squealing in the background now, and Morgan wished they would stop so she could hear what she was listening for. She relaxed her lips, and Ford relaxed his. He smiled, not like Ford but like Ford if he had loved her. She was touched and kissed him again. "I think you better come inside," she heard Mom say. But, no, that was Tracy's voice. "Come on, you've been out long enough."

Oh, just leave them alone, Morgan thought.

"OK," Tracy said. "But I know Rob wants kids." She stuck her tongue out at Morgan and tramped away through the deep snow with great satisfaction. She was smoking a cigarette and had long blond hair.

Mom? Morgan asked, though she didn't say it out loud. A phone was ringing inside the house.

"Go there!" Ford said and then laughed. Morgan turned toward him, wondering why he didn't sing it. She found that he didn't sing it because he wasn't Ford anymore. He was Rob. He was laughing hard.

He finally sobered up under her hard glare, and then he sneered. "Go ahead. Go there! See what it gets you."

And then all she wanted was to run after Mom, through the deep snow, but she was gone. Answering the phone. And she was Tracy besides. But Morgan ran anyway, or tried to, and tumbled into the snow sculpture, which crumbled beneath her weight as if it were a gentle drift.

"It's not my fault!" Morgan heard a young voice say—the six-year-old

Morgan. "I didn't do anything!" The little Morgan took her dark chocolate eyes and brown curls and ran away. That wasn't Morgan. "Sleepers, Awake!" still played far away through the open back door. It was gray now and warmer, the snow all around shades of slate and charcoal. Morgan looked up and saw crimson petals swirling down on currents she couldn't yet feel. It was the storm she was supposed to predict. That storm—Dad's painting she was supposed to save. How could she have forgotten? And this wasn't the first time.

She struggled to get up from the ruins of the snow sculpture, but she kept slipping. The red petals were snagged by the trees—she had to get to her instruments, to her computer, find out where this was heading, find out what could defuse the weather. Rob was standing nearby, not angry anymore. He smiled and offered his hand like there was nothing wrong.

"We should build a snowman," he said.

Morgan took his hand and then slapped him with the other hand as soon as she was up. His smile infuriated her. Didn't he know the world was ending and she had things to do—things to save?

Dad, what do I do? She tried to shout, but nothing came out. *Can't you tell me what's wrong at least?* She knew he was around somewhere. The phone had stopped ringing. He had to be there. "Sleepers, Awake!" He was there, that's why it was playing on the radio.

"What's wrong?" She got the words out of her mouth at last, and she woke up in her living room.

Dad's reply was in her ears as if the sound waves were fresh in the air. "You're asking me?"

"Well, who am I supposed to ask?" Morgan said, exasperated and exhausted. The only answer was from the radio, the decaying final note of what sounded like a concerto grosso. In the silent seconds before the announcer started to speak, it seemed like she heard Dad say, "Who's left?" But it was her own voice.

Rob's left, she thought, not knowing whether it meant he was gone or still there.

*   *   *

The snapshot of the snow sculpture was in Morgan's purse, plucked from the shoebox in her studio closet. She needed to show it to Rob. It would tell her something. Him something. She would tell him something.

As she stepped out onto the porch, Morgan felt the humidity, a breath of spring saturating the wintry air without alleviating the cold. The temperature was right around freezing, and if there had been sun, the radiant energy would have melted some of the ice and snow. But the sky was gray, nimbostratus as far as the eye could see and farther. It threatened a cold, soaking rain. Her gloved hands felt exposed, and her joints ached with cold.

There were no cars in Tracy's driveway, no kids playing in the yard. "She could be anywhere," Morgan said to herself without realizing she said it aloud or said it at all. Not anywhere, she thought. Not with two small kids in tow. She hoped it wouldn't be just anywhere.

"Any of us could be anywhere," Ford seemed to say from somewhere in her mind. "The possibilities are endless."

OK, Morgan, she told herself. You're going to see Rob. That's it. That's all.

*   *   *

Ten years before, almost to the day, 26-year-old Morgan had found that her bruised right hand could still play the harpsichord. She had tried playing only a couple of days after Callie had slammed into her, and much to her relief, she could handle a basso continuo, though she had to forego some of the fancier ornaments since the pain interfered with the dexterity of her fourth finger. That wasn't a big problem—ornaments were practically by definition nonessential. What bothered her more was that it hurt to hold a tuning hammer. She could tune up a few errant strings, but she didn't have the stamina to re-tune the entire harpsichord after it had been moved to the recital hall for the Monteverdi concert.

But a few other people in town could tune the instrument to mean-tone temperament, and it hadn't been difficult to find one. This evening's rehearsal—the first in the recital hall—went better than she had expected, though it did run long. Over three hours long in fact. That was because the singers had a few problems adjusting to the new temperament. A couple of chorus members had perfect pitch and insisted on singing the "correct" pitches. Why anyone so narrow-minded would even want to do a concert with the Early Music Society, Morgan couldn't fathom. But she liked to think Monteverdi had won them over in the end—those pure thirds were luminous. Tonight she had heard some of the lushest overtones in her experience, a veritable aurora of sympathetic vibrations.

Morgan hadn't spoken to Jana since her injury, but now, as the rehearsal ended, they exchanged nods and smiles. Jana seemed embarrassed and busied herself with placing her gamba in its case. Morgan decided not to ask about Callie. The girl wasn't at rehearsal tonight, and Morgan was determined not to be worried about it.

Pulling on her down parka and mittens, Morgan couldn't help but feel a bit smug. A few people had winter coats, but most of her fellow musicians were pulling windbreakers over their T-shirts, and several were wearing shorts. It had been an especially balmy first day of spring, and when rehearsal began, the sun was just setting and the temperature still clung to 60 degrees. A few people had laughed at her serious winter gear when they saw her come in, but more of them looked worried. "You really should check a weather report before heading out," Morgan replied to the overtly questioning looks. It wasn't like the forecasters were trying to keep the storm a secret.

A moderate low pressure system creeping eastward along the Canadian border was wheeling a mass of dry arctic air through the Midwest with enough energy to stir up some significant snow and wind as it hit the humid springtime air. There would be some snow on the ground and even more in the air by midnight, and school kids might just get a snow day tomorrow. Though she didn't expect much accumulation by the time they got out of rehearsal, the wind chills would make most of her companions pretty uncomfortable if they had to walk more than a block home.

She heard the wind as she walked down the corridor toward the lobby, a low moaning as it hit the northwest corner of the recital hall. It howled when a strong gust pounded the walls and exploded under the building's cornices. Morgan was surprised at its strength, and her fingers began to ache as if with cold. Six blocks home after crossing the parking lot, she thought. She lived east of the recital hall, so the wind would be partly at her back. It shouldn't be too bad, but she wished she had brought her scarf, and she promised herself a hot bath before bed.

As she rounded the corner into the lobby, she gasped and stood still.

The two-story wall of glass looked out onto a thick mass of snow flying horizontally past the dim glowing circles of light that were supposed to illuminate the parking lot.

It seemed that most of the snow was in the air, though it had been coming down for some time. Drifts were forming where the lobby angled away from the rest of the building, and Morgan could see about two inches of snow clinging to the western sides of parked cars. She guessed the north sides were plastered with snow too, though she couldn't see them. The wall was lined with musicians carrying their instruments and scores, shivering at the scene outside, shaking their heads. Several people were talking into their cell phones.

Morgan thought about calling Rob to pick her up. She didn't relish the thought of the walk home, but she didn't want Rob to go out into the storm in his old Ford Focus with the worn tires. Visibility was low, but she could see well enough to navigate the streets on foot, and once she got past the parking lot, there would be more shelter from the wind if she chose the right streets. It was more dangerous to drive, she decided, and since she was dressed for a winter trek, she took a deep breath, opened the door, and headed out across the parking lot.

This was a much stronger storm than had been forecast. She suspected the strength of the jet stream had been underestimated. The resulting upward motion in the atmosphere would have intensified the low pressure at the surface. That, in turn, would have driven the cold front through the Midwest even faster than expected and brought about this quick drop in temperature—it had to be around 20 now. My God, she thought, almost 40 degrees in less than three hours. More than just her fellow musicians would be taken unawares. Someone was going to die tonight, some unprepared motorist blown off the road with no winter coat on hand. A 50-mile-per-hour gust hit her, and she stumbled.

She caught her balance and stepped closer to the nearest row of cars. They didn't afford much protection from the wind, but at least she could grab onto them if she was knocked off-balance again. She flexed her fingers inside her woolen mittens, holding her scores tight under her arm, and breathed slowly and deliberately to keep from panicking. She wasn't in any real danger, she knew that. Only six blocks, and she'd walk most of the way along Grove Avenue with its two blocks of new townhouses built on the north side of the street, close to the sidewalk.

She just needed to get to the edge of the parking lot, cross College Avenue, and duck down Weaver for a block. And Weaver had plenty of windbreaks.

She ran out of cars before she ran out of parking lot. One car was parked away from the others at the end of the row, an old dark Cavalier with the windows frosted up. She angled away from it, following the shortest path to College Avenue. Funny, someone parking an old car like that so far away from the building. It's almost always a new car, owner afraid it would get dinged. But what was really strange was the frost. How had that happened with all this wind? That car must have been there earlier than the others, Morgan thought as she made her way toward the street. Got some frost on it before the storm hit. But that didn't make any sense—the wind would've picked up before the temperature dropped to freezing, and besides, all the cars in the lot had been there before the storm. It took her several more paces to realize: the car had to be frosted from the inside. There was someone or something inside that breathed.

Morgan ran toward the old car, the impact of her boots against the pavement jarring her ankles. A few pages of her bedraggled score escaped from under her arm and caught the wind, but she didn't stop. She tried to peer into the back seat of the car, but she couldn't see much. The clear corners of the windows gave a very limited picture inside. She pounded on the windows, wanting and not wanting an answer. Through a clear spot in the windshield, she caught a view between the front seats, a small tennis-shoed foot dangled from a bare leg, not quite touching the floor, blue in the muffled light of the snow-filled air. The foot was dead still.

After pounding several more times, Morgan ran back to the recital hall, the howling wind tearing her hood from her head. She could see about twenty people through the glass walls, staring out, heads shaking, mouths laughing in disbelief. She was almost to the door when she saw Jana round the corner into the lobby, left hand carrying her gamba case, right hand flipping her hair out of the neckhole of the light sweatshirt she'd put on over her blouse.

Jana's tired smile transmuted into horror. "Oh my God!" she said and dropped her gamba. She tore across the lobby, stopping only to fight with the heavy glass door that didn't want to yield to the wind. She ran past Morgan, and Morgan stopped and looked after her, not knowing whether to run inside to call an ambulance or to follow Jana, offer her mittens, give Callie her coat.

Jana was at the car, fumbling with her keys in the cold and wind, when Morgan decided to head back into the parking lot. She thought she heard Jana's voice, trembling and cracked. "Callie? Oh my God. Callie!" Then the car door slammed, and Jana was attempting to start the cold engine. An irritable cough sputtered out. A higher-tempo cranking rattled on for a few moments more and died. Morgan had almost reached the car when Jana's third try fired up and the car jerked forward. Jana raced the engine and peeled away for the parking lot exit. She sped along College Avenue going about 50 and turned the corner at Clark Street, hardly slowing down. *She can't see out the windshield*, Morgan protested in her mind. *She'll kill someone on her way to the hospital.*

She wanted to follow, but there was no way she could get that far on foot, and she felt unable even to get back into the recital hall. But she did get there, without any clear idea of how. Someone had picked up Jana's viola da gamba from the floor and set it on a bench. A lot of people were waiting for rides, oblivious to Jana and Callie, life and death.

"You OK, Morgan?" some voice asked.

She shook her head and sat down on the bench next to Jana's gamba. She searched her pockets for her phone and opened it up. The signal wouldn't be strong, but she didn't want to text. She needed to hear Rob's voice.

When he picked up, his "Hi, Morgan" echoed.

She didn't have any words at first.

"Morgan? What's up?" His voice continued to echo, its note of concern multiplying.

She started to cry. "It's Callie," she said, trying to explain.

"Morgan? I think you're breaking up." *Breaking up, breaking up.*

"Come," she choked out at last, "please come and get me."

"OK. I'll be right there. Morgan? Just hang on." *Hang on, hang on.*

There were so many reasons she loved Rob, and it made her cry all the harder.

"I'm heading out of the lab right now." *Right now, right now.* "I'll probably lose the signal in the stairwell." *In the stairwell, stairwell.* "I'll be there in five minutes ..."

"Be careful, Rob," she whispered, but she didn't think he heard. There was only silence on the other end now.

She closed her phone and tried to stop crying. Her score was still under her arm. She took it out and leafed through it, trying to identify which pages had flown away in the wind. She loved the yellowed paper, the purity of the black notes dancing on the staves. Her bruised and cold fingers itched even now to follow them over the harpsichord's keys.

It wasn't right, the power these sounds have. Their enthralling mathematical beauty. The precision of thought and action, the perfection—the impossibility—they demanded. It wasn't right.

This shouldn't have been predictable.

The wind was howling outside, but inside it was muffled, like a mother's voice must be to a child in the womb. She tried not to listen.

Rob would be all right. She had told him that morning that he would need his winter coat. He would be all right in the howling wind.

He would be there soon, and that would be enough. He wouldn't leave her, not tonight. It would have to be enough.

*   *   *

Now, 10 years after the Equinox Blizzard, Morgan pulled into the Wolverton State campus a half hour after leaving her house. Her hands were warm, and her thoughts optimistic. She would find Rob. In his lab or his office. Probably alone, maybe with colleagues. Immersed in work, happy to take a break with her. She'd show him the picture, tell him a story he'd never heard before. And he might tell her a story about his mother or maybe his grandfather, who always put him in his place. They would understand that they still had each other. And that was enough.

The weather wasn't cooperating with her optimism, however. It was cold, and the Engineering Quad acted as a wind tunnel, narrowing and focusing the light breezes into buffeting gusts. The clammy air pressed through Morgan's leather gloves and turned her hands to sluggish ice by the time she gripped the door to the new lab wing of Engineering 4. The air inside was dry and warm. She tugged off her gloves and wiggled her fingers in the warmth as she headed up the stairs to the second floor.

Rob's lab was at the end of the new wing, just before the walls changed from large masonry blocks to plaster and red brick. She liked his lab with one wall of exposed brick lined with a wide counter that had a sink at one end. It was a large room that Rob shared with two colleagues, set up for testing soil and treating building materials. The last time she had been here, the place reeked of asphalt—a sample had just been poured and was being compacted with an experimental pressure treatment. Today, it didn't look like anyone was inside. The gray spring light flooded the place from the two large windows on the wall opposite the door, silhouetting the rubber hoses and chemical hoods. Rob's section of the lab was farther down, and she went to the next door.

Several pieces of equipment were on the work bench, shrouded in tarps of cloudy vinyl. Tall lab stools lined up like soldiers beneath the bench. The work areas were pristine. It gave Morgan a shiver, as if Rob had never been there, as if his life had been a lie.

She protested the shiver. Rob always cleaned up his work area when he finished, just as he always swept the front porch when it snowed.

She opened the lab door and was accosted by a familiar smell, though not the smell she expected. Instead of asphalt, tar, burnt metal, or loamy earth, something struck her far more deeply, something dredged up from the silt of her childhood memories. Fels-Naptha, that brown soap Dad used to wash his hands after working in his studio.

She felt a profound sense of loss.

She hadn't known that engineers used Fels-Naptha, though it made sense. If it worked for the hands of painters, it was no doubt good for hands that tested soil samples or the various kinds of chemical sludge they used on road surfaces. As she turned back toward the door, she caught sight of a worn brown soap bar at the sink. And next to it, a bottle of Turpenoid.

Lightning leaped between her head and heart, freezing her in stark bright clarity. Where there was Turpenoid, there was oil paint.

Rob had another life, a life he was keeping her out of.

The bright, clear, and blinding light faded.

So Rob was painting. So what? It wasn't like he was having an affair.

She closed the lab door and headed down the hall. She thought she smelled linseed oil, and its distinctive trace grew stronger as she turned the corner into the older part of the building where Rob's office was. His door was open. Hazy shadows played on the floor before the threshold, animated in the bright gray light that Morgan knew came from the large window behind Rob's desk.

As she approached, she heard a high voice laugh—musical tinkling laughter, the sound of someone having fun. She stood, stock still, blinded once more by a detail of Rob's hidden life.

She took slow and deep breaths, willed her heart to stop beating so violently, and the blinding light eased its stranglehold. She pulled her hair back from her forehead and focused her hearing beyond the hum of the building's HVAC system to the conversation in Rob's office.

"Yes, I see what you mean," the woman's voice said. "He must have been a wonderful teacher. I can see his influence, especially in that piece there. But you certainly have your own distinct vocabulary. That looks like the one Walter liked—is it?"

Morgan didn't hear Rob reply. Maybe he nodded.

"I wouldn't be surprised if he made you an offer on it."

Rob laughed. "I wouldn't know what to say. Never thought I'd impress the boss that way!"

"So how did you meet Jon Tallis' daughter? She's an artist too, I suppose?"

"No," Rob said, and Morgan felt the air catch in her throat on its way to her lungs. "She's a meteorologist. We met in grad school."

"Is that so! Who would've thought! A meteorologist? What a shame."

Rob laughed. Laughed! "It's a pretty important job. She's really good at it. It's pretty visual too, you know." He sounded defensive. Maybe the laugh had been nervousness. "She's a musician too. Piano and harpsichord. Mostly piano these days." He sounded disappointed. Yes, that was definitely disappointment. "She plays professionally."

"Ah, so she *is* an artist."

Rob didn't say anything. Maybe he nodded.

Maybe he shook his head.

Morgan stared at the gray terrazzo floor and renewed her grip on her hair.

"Now, this one," the woman said, apparently looking at a new painting, "this is interesting."

No one said anything for a moment.

"It's reminiscent of a landscape," the woman went on, "but very personal, almost sexual."

Rob sort of snickered—it was the noise he made when he wanted to ignore a comment while seeming to respond to it.

"Was this inspired by a topographical map, like that other one?"

"No, actually," Rob said and cleared his throat. "I was looking at a snowdrift in the back yard, and light from some car headlights raked across it, and the shadows…." He trailed off, sounding very sad. Maybe the woman encouraged him with a look, maybe she touched his arm in sympathy, but he went on as he seldom did unprompted. "I liked the form, the curves of the snowbank, the low-angle light—jagged, you know. So I guess I decided to take it and make it warm. Friendlier."

"Interesting. I'd say it was warmer than friendly." She laughed, almost a giggle. She thought he was lying, it occurred to Morgan. She thought it was a body. Maybe the woman was right. Whose? Morgan wanted to see the painting, and her heart began to beat furiously again. It wasn't right that Rob hadn't shown it to her, hadn't mentioned it to her, hadn't mentioned that he was painting to her.

"Do you and your wife have children?" the woman asked, voice silky smooth, light and high, like a well-trained soprano.

"No, I'm afraid not."

Don't sound so apologetic, Morgan protested, even as tears stung her eyes. She saw Callie lunging across the rehearsal hall, music stands toppling over. She saw Emilia dragging on a cigarette, looking for a reaction.

"I sometimes wish we did," Rob said.

Anger balled up in Morgan's throat and made it hard to breathe.

"Well, you're still young!" the high voice laughed. "You and your wife really must have some." As if children were something you could sample at a dinner party. "It would be a shame if you didn't pass on Jon's legacy—and your own!"

The anger in Morgan's throat became too charged not to ignite. "You don't have kids just so they can carry on." Her voice sounded remarkably cool and soft for a thunderbolt. She was standing in the doorway.

"Morgan!" Just what kind of surprise was in Rob's voice, Morgan couldn't be sure. It sounded like delight, but when she glanced at his face, he looked frightened. Guilty.

The woman was much older than Morgan, maybe in her 60s. She was tall with short graying blond hair and high cheekbones accentuated by makeup. She was a dramatic figure, dressed in black—a draping black chenille sweater over black jeans. High black boots with scuff marks and salt stains and a worn stacked heel. Around her neck was a long, brilliant silk scarf of many colors.

"And this is Jon Tallis' daughter! We met 20-odd years ago in Indianapolis. You frowned at me then just like you're doing now!"

That was meant to be disarming, which Morgan found irritating. "I'm afraid I don't remember."

Rob stepped in. "Morgan, this is Nadine Rohnsfeldt, a painter from the art department. She's a big fan of Dad's—"

"Yes, I heard as I was coming down the hall. I remember Indianapolis now. Your name. You had that large painting with lots of vermillion in the show. *Fevered Pitch*. Dad kept trying to find something musical in it. 'Pitch'—he thought it should have a musical meaning. I thought it looked more like tree sap than sound." She tried to make this sound like an insult, but Professor Rohnsfeldt just laughed that high tinkling sound that Morgan might have found pleasant under other circumstances.

"Morgan has a formidable memory," Rob said, in that cautionary voice that sounded eager and conversational to everyone else.

"It's an astute observation," Professor Rohnsfeldt said. "I did tend toward the botanical in those days."

Morgan continued to scowl and stared at the easel set up on a drop cloth to the left of Rob's big wooden desk. It faced away from her, toward the large window. Several small paintings stood upright on the floor, but she couldn't see them well.

"Nadine's a friend of Anne Taney's," Rob was saying. "You know, Walter's wife?"

"Yes, I remember Anne."

"Walter saw Rob's soil and climate painting, and he couldn't stop talking about it at dinner last week," Professor Rohnsfeldt said, this time without laughing, as if she'd finally accepted the chill in Morgan's voice. "So I just had to see it myself. Rob's been showing me his other work." When Morgan didn't say anything, she picked up her coat from a hook next to the door. Black. Very nice wool. "Thanks, Rob. You have to keep painting. Could I stop by again to see what you're doing?"

"Sure. Thanks for the encouragement." Was that note of reproach intentional? "Maybe we could see some of your work."

"Of course! Come by my studio—anytime Tuesday and Thursday

mornings this semester. You're welcome too, Morgan. It was nice to see you again," she said from the door. "I'm—sorry for your loss. And I apologize for the comment about having children." So she was more observant than most, Morgan thought. "Overstepping my bounds as usual."

Morgan nodded and tightened the corners of her mouth. She couldn't see Professor Rohnsfeldt's face because she was blinking to prevent tears from falling. She looked down at the faux Persian rug Rob used to cover the scrapes in the hardwood floors.

Rob took three steps toward her and stopped two feet away. She could make out the watery outline of his brown boots. She felt his hand under her chin, as if to lift her face. She swatted it away and jerked her head up. The worry in his eyes and forehead wasn't enough to temper her anger.

"Sorry," he said. "I just don't know what to do."

She glared at him, unable to say anything, unable even to snarl.

Rob sighed and crossed his arms. "I've been painting." He stepped back and motioned toward the easel with his head. "Probably more than I should. Though I still get some research in." He waited a moment, then backed up farther and half-leaned, half-sat on the edge of his desk. "It's going pretty well, considering. Thanks for asking."

He was outside of striking range. And she would have had to take too many steps to get to him, and she was afraid her energy would dissipate. She needed it for something, but she couldn't remember for what.

"Walter stopped in a few weeks ago," Rob went on, "wondering what the funny smell in the hallway was. Linseed oil—haven't thought of it as a funny smell for years. I was afraid he'd tell me to knock it off, you know. First kicked out of the house, then out of my office. But he actually liked the painting I was working on."

Still, Morgan said nothing. Not that she didn't want to—she just didn't have the words. She wanted to tell him off, accuse him of something, and though she felt naked and betrayed, she couldn't make any logical connection to anything he'd said or done. It was still his fault—if only she could find the detail, the clue she could follow until the next flash of lightning showed her what it was.

"So what are you doing here, Morgan? You caught me red-handed. Though why my painting should bother you, I'll never understand." He sat farther back on his desk. "Are you checking up on me? You're looking at me like I was having an affair or something."

"Funny you should bring that up," Morgan spat out, as if the words were ready-made, already born, already hanging on the air.

"What? So that's why you're here? Well, so sorry to disappoint you, but I'm as trustworthy as ever."

"Trustworthy? When you hide everything from me? When you talk behind my back, look down on me, confide in Tracy—"

"Tracy? I don't 'confide' in Tracy!"

"She seems to think you do."

"For crying out loud, the kid has a crush on me." He shook his head and looked away.

It was as if he'd confessed to a heinous crime, the next bolt of lightning struck her so deep inside. She felt like she couldn't possibly have any breath left, but somehow she was speaking. "And whose fault is that? A married woman—with two kids!—doesn't get a crush on a man unless he's giving her something."

"Giving her what? There's nothing between Tracy and me. She's young, she's lonely, she's bored, and her husband travels. A woman like that will get a crush on any man who gives her a kind look."

"A kind look? Kind words?" Her hands were tingling with shock. "A kind touch?" She knew how it worked. Hadn't she observed Ford for years? "The sympathetic pat on the shoulder, the friend-in-need handholding?"

"No! Do you think I'm an idiot?" He looked as if he expected an answer. But he didn't give her time to think of one. "She might've tried that on me, but I wasn't going to fall for it. In fact, when I didn't a few nights ago, she threw a cup of hot coffee on me."

"Oh, that's what happened to the yellow shirt? It's a good story. So good, if it were true, I would've heard it already."

"And maybe you would have, if you gave any indication of being interested!"

She couldn't look at him anymore, but she couldn't leave either. She stood there, her hands shaking, her eyes searching the floor without any goal.

After a few moments, Rob took a deep breath. "This isn't about Tracy," he said, and he stepped toward her. "Is it?" He took another step closer and leaned toward her, searching her face. "Is it? Because it makes no sense. How long has she lived next door? If I'd been the least bit attracted to her, you would've known it long before now."

"I'm talking about now," she shot back, fixing him in her sights again, "not—not—before. Don't tell me you don't know that things are different. Things are different."

"Yeah. Things are different. That's my point. Between us, things are different. And it doesn't have anything to do with Tracy. As far as I'm concerned, there's no attraction at all." He gave out a short snort and looked to the side. "Other than a couple of cute kids."

Her hand flew toward his face with the entire force of her being behind it.

Rob's reaction was as instinctive and immediate as hers. His eyes widened in surprise, and he pinned both of her arms to her sides. His face was red, and his voice was soft and strained. "The other thing about Tracy that I might think was attractive is that she talks to me. At least I know where I stand. Why the hell don't you talk to me? What the hell is wrong?" His eyes filled with tears, and he squeezed her arms until they hurt, shook her in small jerks as if they were bursts of energy that escaped his control. "Yell at me if you want. Use whatever foul language you want, but talk to me. Please."

Morgan felt hot tears on her cheeks, angry tears that burned her nose and eyes. She wanted to talk, but there were no words. She couldn't remember why she came here—no, it had something to do with a photograph. She saw the black and white of the snow sculpture in her mind, wanted to get the image out of her purse, show it to him, show him something. But she didn't know what it meant. And he was holding her arms.

But Rob, he didn't understand, he thought she was just being obstinate. He tightened his lips in a thin line and shook his head. Then he let go, pushing her away as he did. He turned his back to her and said, "How can you do this to me? All we have is each other."

She heard scorn in his voice. Accusation. "You can't blame me for that," she cried through her confusion. "We both agreed. We both agreed!"

He turned around, wary, and watched her. "What do you think I'm blaming you for?"

She was pacing in small steps, as if she were in a cage. "It was enough!" she shouted. "Just the two of us. We agreed!"

Rob's eyebrows were high but trying to squeeze together, that look of confusion and hope he had when he was trying hard to figure something out. As if he could still get what he wanted.

"You think I haven't given anything up?" she demanded. "I see the snow in the backyard without a mark on it—I haven't made a snowball in years!" Why couldn't she stand still? Why couldn't she hold her ground, stand firm? She stopped and tried to fix her glare on Rob, show him she was in control. But the tears got in the way, and it frustrated her. "I see it all the time," she said, pacing again. "Jana couldn't control Callie, Isabel can't control Emilia, and then there's Tracy—she can't even buckle Mac into his car seat right—and there she is, throwing it in my face that *we* don't have a family. Then there's this Nadine rattlehead professor, saying we have to have kids because of Dad, and just who took care of her kids, I wonder, when she was out making a goddamn name for herself?"

"Morgan, it's OK!" Rob reached out to her. To calm her down. He should have been apologizing.

"It's OK? It's OK to blame me for being responsible. I was just trying to do the right thing. And *you* agreed. We'd have each other you said, we'd have our work, and that would be enough for us. Enough to last."

Though she could only make out the watery outline of his expression, Morgan saw Rob's confusion evaporate. He shook his head slowly, as if he were viewing an unexpected wonder for the first time. He smiled and said, "So that's what this is about!"

She almost screamed in frustration. "This?" As if a four-letter generic word could sum up everything she was feeling? "I don't know what *this* is about. OK? I don't fucking know. But I know I'm sick of you always thinking there's an answer, looking down on me for not trying hard enough!"

He opened his mouth to say something, but she couldn't stand the thought of what might come out. She turned, tripped on the rug, and stumbled out of the room, the sound of her missteps drowning any protest Rob might have offered.

Rob

Of course I wanted to run after her—I'd figured it out! But I was smiling, like I'm smiling now, and that would only make her angry.

Jana couldn't control Callie, that's what Morgan said. I haven't heard those names in years, but I do remember them. Morgan had talked about Callie a lot the year before we got married—poor little hyperactive kid who never got enough attention. Wreaked havoc wherever she went. Too much energy and no control over it. That's how I remember her, though I never met her. She slammed Morgan into the harpsichord at a rehearsal, and it bruised her hand, drew blood even. She didn't get her dexterity back for weeks. Still, Morgan worried about her a lot more than she blamed her.

The big storm came not long after that. The Equinox Blizzard, that's what they called it. It had to have a name, not because it was so big but because it was so sudden. The temperature dropped something like 40 degrees in a couple of hours, and that's what made it deadly. Spring had sprung two weeks before, and suddenly it was winter again, and people didn't expect it.

Jana didn't expect it, and Callie paid the price. I tried to tell Morgan, you can only forecast the storms, you can't make people listen to the forecasts, but she still felt responsible. As if she should have paid attention to the signs, seen it coming. It was an awful shock to her, discovering Callie in a car at the edge of the parking lot. She didn't make any sense when she called me that night. I just knew something was terribly wrong and I had to come get her. I found her in the lobby, looking at her hand, really concentrating on it, like she was trying to read something in the bruises Callie had given her.

She said we had to go to the hospital, said it in a small voice that broke apart, and it wasn't until we were in the car and on our way that I realized it wasn't for her. "Callie," she said. "Callie's dead, I think."

She sounded hollow, like she was talking across a long distance inside.

Callie wasn't dead though. The police were talking to Jana when we got to the hospital. She looked over at us, and when she saw Morgan, her eyes got very wide for just a second, then she looked down, away from us. The police looked over their shoulders in our direction, and Morgan turned and held on to me. The emergency room was busy. Car accidents. We just looked like any other worried couple. The police didn't question us.

They took Callie away from Jana of course. Jana had drugged the girl before locking her in the car. She had done it more than once too. The girl lost a couple of toes to frostbite or something like that. It was in the papers. Morgan read every word but never wanted to talk about it. But I know it scared her. Hell, it scared me.

We talked a lot that summer about kids. Whether we should have a family. I held on to the dream longer than she did.

"Nothing's perfect, Morgan. No child gets everything they need, but we all survive. We all thrive."

"That's the point, Rob. Nothing's perfect. Something's got to give. What's it going to be? My music? I can't do it, Rob. I'd try, and I'd fail, just like Jana. It's just not right to fail your children."

"But you're not in this alone. I'd be there, we'd do it together."

"Cold comfort, we'd fail together. Can you honestly say you'd give up your long hours at the lab for 10 years or so, right at the time when you're expected to be gunning for tenure?"

I had to admit she was right, and eventually I did. I was scared, and she was right. "I trust your judgment," I said. I meant it too. It was an act of trust, not blame, but she didn't want to accept it.

"No! You should have children, Rob." She had tears in her eyes, and I suddenly realized what she was thinking. She wouldn't let me interrupt. "You were meant to have a family, and I wasn't."

"We were meant to be together!" I took hold of her shoulders and wouldn't let her turn away. "That's all I'm sure of, Morgan."

She kept shaking her head. "I can't deprive you of a family. You'd blame me. Maybe not right away, but you'd hate me eventually."

"The thought of not having kids—sure, it makes me sad, but it's a relief too. I don't want kids if we can't do right by them."

She laid her head on my chest and held on tight, but she didn't say anything.

"I want *our* life," I said, "not the life people think we're supposed to have. It's enough, just the two of us. More than enough—more than anyone has any right to expect."

We made the right decision. We didn't even miss having a family. We *were* a family! Until we started failing each other.

OK, I've had some regrets. Lately. Maybe thinking about Dad. His legacy, like Nadine said, maybe I have been thinking about that. But I've never blamed Morgan. Never. It never even occurred to me.

But it must have occurred to her. It occurred to her all those years ago. Does she think I've been throwing it in her face? Every time I talk about Tracy, every time I talk about Dad? That fight we had over Dad's paints—is that why she was so angry? When I was talking about purity, did she think I was talking about sterility? I mean, I was—but I was talking about art!

Oh, Morgan. Nothing's ever simple, is it?

When I think there's a chance we could have children, that the possibility is out there, the glimmer of hope flickering in my chest feels an awful lot like fear. When I think the opportunity is past, I feel that same relief I felt 10 years ago. The same sadness.

People think of honesty as straight, on the mark, yes or no. Clear and linear. But honesty is a mess. Almost by definition, you can't engineer it. Simplicity is easier, but it just pretends to be correct when it's just more arbitrary. Nothing's ever simple. That's the honest truth that Morgan knows but doesn't always have the patience for.

The first time I remember her saying that, *Nothing's ever simple*, it was about Ford of all things, that tenor who's been coming on to her for the better part of a decade. Over the years we've had a lot of laughs at his expense, but it really bugged me when she first met him—I think it was around the time of the Equinox Blizzard in fact. He was in that concert. He's older than we are, 10 years or so. She used to come home and laugh about him flirting with her. I finally got sick of it and told her I was going to start picking her up after rehearsal.

"That's crazy," she said. She was getting ready for bed. I was already under the covers. "You're never done at the lab before 10."

"Then stop talking to this guy who keeps coming on to you. How do you think it makes me feel?"

She stopped in the middle of buttoning up her pajama top, opened her mouth and shut it again. Then she shook her head.

"What? You think I like the thought of other men trying to seduce you?"

She burst out laughing, as if she'd just gotten a joke. "I didn't know you were so insecure. I mean, really. Why would you care? You really think he'd have any chance?"

"Well, no, I don't think you'd sleep with Ford."

"You can be sure of it." She leaned over and kissed me. Confidently. "Nothing's ever simple, Rob."

"What do you mean?"

"A cause doesn't have just one possible effect. A guy comes on to me—it doesn't mean anything will happen." She shook her head again, impatiently. "Ford is who he is. And he's harmless. So decide not to worry about it. It's the simplest thing."

I laughed. "You just said nothing's ever simple."

"It's not. But that's no reason not to make a decision."

"I don't understand."

"Neither do I. But we don't have to." She hadn't finished buttoning her top, and she glanced down at her chest as if considering whether she should. "The gaps in understanding make life interesting."

"So life is a project with too many degrees of freedom to ever analyze."

"And even when you do"—and here she flashed her sharp teeth at me—"you end up three 64ths short of an octave." Then she bit my ear.

I still don't know exactly what she meant. But she didn't know either. We didn't have the simple truth, and it didn't matter. The simple truth, that's a falsehood. That's what's been killing us.

Eight

Morgan pulled into the Wolverton Civic Center parking lot, controlling her turn with admirable skill, considering her exhaustion and the freezing drizzle that coated the pavement. The precipitation had started earlier than was forecast, and it was supposed to be snow this far north, turning to rain as a warm front passed through later in the day. The freezing drizzle was an important detail, not to mention a dangerous one, and she considered calling it in. She had other things clouding her mind, however. Besides, she knew the Wolverton city police were very good about reporting hazardous weather.

Her phone had buzzed several times on the drive over. She pulled it out of her purse and saw two texts and a voicemail from Rob. She put it back without reading or listening to them.

She wondered why she had come to the Civic Center. She told herself that she wanted to see how *Peter Grimes* was shaping up with the orchestra, and if anyone were to ask her, that's what she would reply. Idle curiosity was a good enough excuse, but on some level she was aware it wasn't the truth.

She didn't want to go home just then. She didn't want to see the blank wall in the foyer, Dad's Steinway in the living room. She didn't want to be reminded of the neglected harpsichord upstairs, of Rob's presence and absence all around.

She stepped out of the car and slipped, flying out flat underneath her car door, smacking her head on the car as she went down. She felt the barely frozen ice deciding to be water under her body. It seeped through her jeans and into her hair. Her wool hat had flipped off her head and landed on her face, so she saw little beyond gray light in the crevices of the knitted yarn. She removed the hat from her face and saw the uniform sky framed by the car and door. The rain fell on her face, cold but liquid, even as it froze on contact with every surface around her. She wished the rain would freeze over her as well in a clear hard shell, wished she was so cold that the terrible heat of her anger and grief would subside.

But that wouldn't happen, and she knew she would just end up wet and sick, without any solace. So she pulled herself to her feet, holding onto the car rather than the door, which might move and throw her to the ground again. She tested her footing, careful to plant her feet at the angle most likely to resist the slipperiness of the parking lot. She felt a sharp burning at the back of her head where it hit the car, but she was reassured that the inventory of her bruises ended there. The pain was all in the back of her head, none in the front, so a concussion wasn't likely. The bump should be iced, but she wasn't in the mood. And she wasn't in the mood to stand in the rain any longer.

The air inside the Civic Center was warm and dry, though the sounds emanating from the auditorium evoked the sea—tons of water, breezes blowing off the swells, an enormous power gathering itself in its own time. The orchestra was playing beautifully, and Morgan slipped into the auditorium and sat in the back row. It was just inside Act II when Isabel, as Ellen Orford, sang to Peter's young apprentice on a Sunday morning, the day of rest. *The treason of the waves glitters like love*, she sang, *glitters like love.* She was singing well, clear and sweet, with a lightness to her tone that radiated innocence. But then it turned subtly toward the cynical, and the arch in her eyebrow reinforced the effect: *Storm and all its terrors are nothing to the heart's despair.* She was supposedly singing to the apprentice, about the apprentice's hard life, about everyone's hard life. But these were words that a little boy wouldn't understand. She was singing to herself and to everyone in the audience who had known heartache. And she was looking off, not at the apprentice, but straight at Morgan, straight at Morgan fainting into a kiss with Ford.

Morgan jerked her head up from a doze. The back of her head hurt. Ford had joined Isabel onstage. He was wearing a plaid flannel shirt, something he wouldn't have been caught dead in offstage. Morgan snickered and felt a small rush of affection for him. He and Isabel were singing a duet, singing very well—and acting well too. They were arguing about how to treat the apprentice, whether he should work or have a day of rest. And behind that, whether Peter's life was redeemable, whether it was right to bring the innocent apprentice into this life of hard and dangerous work, vulnerable to the violence of Peter's tortured mind. Morgan felt their helplessness, their affection for each other, their frustration with each other and with their situation. The little boy who was playing the apprentice, however, he wasn't acting well at all. He looked lost, not reacting at all to what the adults were singing. They were talking about his future! Morgan felt sorry for him—no one seemed to notice him, to give him any direction. He was neglected in this grownup world, and Morgan felt the sting of tears in her eyes at how unfair it was.

All of a sudden, she felt Ford's eyes pick her out in the semidarkness of the empty auditorium. It didn't break his stride, but she felt there was something—something more robust in his tone, more expansive in his gestures. He was showing off, she felt that as keenly as she felt his eye contact. *He works for me, leave him alone, he's mine!* It was the cry of a profoundly frustrated man, claiming what he could, what wasn't his, because he had no claim to what should be his. She felt another swell of affection for Ford and, strangely enough, for Peter.

Now Isabel sang with a dark voice (too dark, Morgan thought). *This unrelenting work, this grey, unresting industry, what aim, what future, what peace will your hard profits buy?* Ellen didn't understand, Morgan protested to herself, she didn't understand that it was all he had left— work, the only way to get through the hopelessness, the rejection, the disappointments. Obligations had to be met, and he had to choose. Ellen was supposed to be on Peter's side, and all she could do was find fault. Ford sang, heartbreaking in its beauty, *My only hope depends on you. If you take it away, what's left?*

Ford was on her side. He was singing for her, standing with her against the world that told her on all sides that she was wrong. And in a flash of clarity she knew. Ford was singing for Dad too—how could she have missed it? But what was the hope? How was she taking it away? Why didn't he tell her? Why was everything so jumbled, meaning always hidden behind something, behind a painting or a song or a dream? Peter dies, so what's right after all is said and done?

So be it! Ford sang, decisive. *And God have mercy upon me!* He exited, grabbing the inept boy and taking him off to his death.

Morgan closed her eyes without realizing it. She followed Ford and the little boy to Peter's hut on the cliff, an upturned boat with a door cut into it. The boy was unhappy but docile as he followed Ford to the hut. The wind was howling and cold, ice pellets beat on the boy's face, but the boy wouldn't go inside. He knew death lay inside shelter. He tried to run away, to twist out of the grip of Ford whose smile was mischievous, playful, as he clung to the boy's small wrist. His left wrist, the one with the scars on it.

Morgan jerked her wrist away from Ford, awake in an instant. Ford had a mischievous smile, just like in the dream. But that was the usual way Ford smiled.

"I saw you from the stage," he said. "What are you doing here? You look like you should be in bed."

Her mouth felt dry and empty. She cleared her throat and found she still had a voice. "Just curious, I guess. To see how it all comes together?" She didn't like the question in her voice. Ford would seize on it.

"I think," he said, putting his hand over hers, "you wanted to see me." He picked up her hand and kissed the palm. She didn't pull away like she knew she should. He looked at her, still mischievous but more alert.

"You're singing well," she said. "Acting well too?"

"Not now," he replied, instantly making sense of her senseless question. His eyes turned serious, as if the key changed from B-flat major to g minor, and he kissed her palm again. Then he kissed her scars and caught his breath.

She was looking at him, as if in a safely distant audience, kissing someone else's scars—such a touching and intimate gesture. He looked at her with deep, shoreless eyes, boundless in their longing and pursuit. It was strangely satisfying, like weather, like a puzzle with infinite variables. She leaned closer to get a better look at it, even though she knew what she would see wasn't allowed.

Ford's smile changed, became less pronounced but not less happy. He spoke rapidly, *sotto voce.* "They'll take a while to get through the next scene with the chorus. Charles has been doing all the chorus scenes twice, even when they're going well—and then of course there's the women's quartet. Meet me in the small studio upstairs. Five minutes?"

Morgan said nothing in reply, just looked at him, hearing his offer. It was fascinating, like the hint of tornadic activity in a burgeoning supercell. The suspense alone was gripping. He squeezed her hand, and she felt the impression of her wedding ring linger between her fingers even after he'd left.

She looked toward the exit on the left, the one he would have gone through, wondering for a moment why he had left so suddenly. Then she remembered—he was going up to the studio. He was meeting somebody.

"Morgan?"

Emilia was standing in the aisle next to her, looking at her with the same curious expression that might have been on Morgan's own face.

"You like Ford, don't you." Emilia didn't seem to be asking a question, but a reply did seem to be in order.

"I've known him a long time." Morgan was proud of the statement's ambiguity. It had the nice fit-together nonsense of a dream.

"But you're married." Emilia wasn't protesting, just observing a fact.

Morgan nodded. "I've known my husband a long time too." It was beginning to seem less dreamlike.

"He kissed your wrist." She might have added, "That's weird."

"Scars," Morgan said, stretching her wrist out of the sleeve of her sweater. Emilia looked frightened but leaned forward, curious. "I cut my wrist a long time ago."

"Are you OK?"

Morgan frowned because she didn't have an answer. She shook her head more in frustration than reply. She got up with purpose, thinking she had somewhere to go and time was of the essence.

*　*　*

Nineteen-year-old Morgan surveyed the utensils in a kitchen drawer at Dad's house as the Weather Channel chatted away at the end of the counter. The meteorologist warned with enthusiasm about the harsh blast of arctic air that would assault the northern Great Lakes tomorrow. Down here they probably wouldn't get much snow that weekend, flurries maybe, but more cold air was on the way. Her injured tendon throbbed under the bandages on her left wrist, and Morgan found she was rubbing her hands as if they were cold. She stopped.

No knives, she thought as she pushed her hair out of her eyes. She wanted to make an apple pie, but there were no knives. Not that there was any risk of her using them on herself—she was getting plenty of sleep these days. Too much sleep, she thought. She made a mental note never to say that to Dad or to the psychiatrist she saw twice a week. She corralled her thoughts back to today's challenge, making an apple pie without a knife. That would have to do until she could tackle Chopin and his "Butterfly" etude again.

She picked out a potato peeler and an apple wedger from the drawer and slammed it shut, jangling and rattling the jumble of metal and plastic inside.

"Morgan? Everything all right in there?" Dad called out from the other end of the house.

How had he heard that with his studio door closed? "Fine, Dad. I'm just baking something."

He didn't answer, and Morgan didn't hear his studio door squeak shut, so she picked up an apple and started to peel it as she waited for him to come into the kitchen to check on her. She didn't think she would have much trouble convincing him that the peeler and wedger weren't lethal weapons. But he didn't come in. Instead, she heard him begin to play a Bach invention. Number 14, a rather strange accompaniment to the Folgers coffee jingle now playing on the Weather Channel. Morgan turned the TV down and continued to peel.

Fourteen was one of their favorites, full of near turns—lots of fun, but as she imagined herself playing it, she winced. The fifth finger of her left hand would get a painful workout in that piece. She thought of alternate fingerings, seeing the score in her mind as she listened to Dad. He took it a little slower than she would, his tempo inconsistent—hard for an amateur to avoid—but the fun expressed in the theme and counterpoint still came through. A conversation between the right hand and the left, one repeating the other, saying the same thing in a slightly different way, like a well-tuned comedy act. Eventually both straight man and comic were talking at once, exactly in rhythm with each other. Of course, they couldn't keep that up forever, so they split up again and finished in a playful round. Bach had a sense of humor, and she didn't understand why everyone always took him so seriously.

Dad was messing up the part where both hands played in unified rhythm. But that didn't surprise her, and she knew it wouldn't frustrate him like it would her. Not like it would frustrate him to miscalculate the proportion of pigments when he was mixing a color or misjudge the angle and curve of a line he was painting. It was one of the things that made her feel safe at home, that they understood one another's frustrations.

He finished the piece in admirable style, and she imagined she could hear him giggling. Then there was only the low chatter of the Weather Channel and the soft wet plop of apple peel dropping into the garbage disposal. Behind that, the door to Dad's studio squeaked shut.

Morgan couldn't remember the last time she'd played number 14 or any invention for that matter. Maybe two years ago? That was hard to believe. But she had been—and soon would be again—too busy with Chopin and Mendelssohn and all those other 19th-century romantics with big hands, too busy trying to prove Leo Neville wrong.

At the thought of Leo Neville, Morgan threw the switch to the garbage disposal, drowning all other sounds in its loud grinding. She imagined with satisfaction that Neville's long-fingered hands were mixed in with the green and red peels of the Macintosh apples. She ought to be grateful to him, she thought in a dubious attempt at charity. Proving him wrong had fueled her drive to succeed as much as caffeine and adrenaline. She had thought of him every time she'd popped a No-Doz.

The familiar low-grade panic that had haunted Morgan for a year began to grow and take form as she stared at the denuded apple resting on the counter. Why was she making a pie? She had to practice—she had wasted enough time coddling that tendon. If she was ever going to make the "Butterfly" fly, she was going to have to start sooner rather than later.

Morgan turned the TV off, interrupting the local forecast she had seen 10 times already, and walked resolutely to the music room. As she moved down the hall, the faint smell of linseed oil grew stronger. Dad would hear her, but he wouldn't stop her. She was confident he understood what she had to do.

*   *   *

Thirty-six-year-old Morgan walked along the upstairs corridor of the Civic Center, past the closed offices, toward the rehearsal studios. Ghostly light came in from the window at the end of the darkened hall, and her rubber-soled footsteps echoed, their squeaks and scuffs lengthening and diffusing into a dream chorus of scurrying creatures. In the background she heard the tinkling laughter of Nadine Rohnsfeldt, as if it were played on a badly tuned harpsichord. Her chest tightened in anticipation of dry lightning. Rob's secret life, she kept thinking. It seemed only fitting to make something to hide from Rob since he was hiding from her. "Hiding," she said and punched the air at her side. She stopped at the sound of her voice, startled with the realization that she wasn't dreaming.

Outside the studio door, she heard a piano start up, very faint behind the soundproofing. It sounded like Chopin.

She opened the door half-expecting to hear the "Butterfly" etude, but instead it was the stormy intro to Peter's brief aria in Act I. Ford began to sing, *What harbour shelters peace, away from tidal waves, away from storms?* She stepped into the room. He continued singing, his clear tenor sounding as full and open as she had ever heard it. *What harbour can embrace terrors and tragedies? With her there'll be no quarrels.*

"That's not an accurate picture of marriage," she said. She closed the door.

Ford laughed and turned his head toward her, hands restless on the keys. "I wouldn't know. And neither would Peter for that matter. I always thought that was the point."

Morgan stood next to him, and he took her left hand and played with her rings. She thought maybe she'd take them off, the wedding band and the diamond, but she decided not to. Betrayal was the point after all. She felt heated inside, as if her heart were filled with scorching desert sand.

Ford was now kissing her fingertips, licking each of them lightly, playfully but with reverence too. He's good, Morgan thought. He played this game very well. He found her right hand and put it behind his neck. Then he closed his eyes, almost, not quite, and breathed out luxuriously for an amazingly long time, as if grateful for a rest after a long wait. Or showing off his lung capacity. Could be either, probably both, she thought. He stood and put his arm around her, pulled his hand through her hair, back from her forehead, as if he wanted her to listen.

She was listening. She heard beats. The beat of her heart, the beat of his, out of sync, out of resonance, a thoroughly impure interval, and that was what she wanted.

He kissed her now, his hand on the back of her head, and it hurt, like it was bruised, but she didn't complain because it felt nice in another way. He tasted her lips and let out a soft moan as if they tasted divine, and he kissed her ear, and she heard herself gasp, and his reaction was immediate. He whispered her name in her ear, as if she'd given him the only gift he'd ever wanted and he was so moved he couldn't say any more. She felt a leap of warmth, not the hot anger burning dry in her chest but a liquid warmth that said yes somewhere deeper, lower. She curled her neck to the side and kissed his neck just behind the jaw. She expected something that didn't happen and felt a vague confusion, though that lovely liquid warmth didn't abate and pulsed on with unequal beats. And she remembered, that's Rob's spot. The arid heat in her chest flared, and the liquid warmth rose to meet it, creating a kind of weather that fed on its own energy. She felt Ford's lips with her fingertips, growled low and bit his ear. He took a deep and forceful breath then bit her fingers. It didn't hurt, but she whined, and he liked that act.

He pressed into her, through their clothes, and together they searched for buttons, buckles, zippers, anything that gave them access to the skin underneath. She pulled his flannel shirt out of his jeans, and they each felt underneath the other's clothes before they started to remove them, impatient and patient at once. Morgan felt the shape of his muscles, the strange proportions, the foreign rhythms, and her anger grew as much as her abandon. Ford breathed in, and his arms weren't around her anymore, they were removing her shirt, and when she was free of it, she saw his face, close to hers and then kissing her again, as hungrily as she found herself kissing him. Then he was talking to her, whispering in her ear. "I wish this could go on forever, but they'll be looking for me soon. Next time—God!" And they both caught their breath. "Next time, we have to take all night."

He had unhooked her bra, and now he separated from her to pull off his jeans and underwear, and she didn't like him so unconnected. She wanted him to undress her, but he was looking for something. She pulled off her bra and meant to remove the loose jeans that were falling away from her hips, unzipped, but he was holding something out to her, between them. His smile was easy, intimate. He was her old friend Ford whom she'd never let get this close before. "Would you like to do the honors, or shall I?"

Her hand touched the condom and froze. She hadn't handled a condom in years. There was a reason for that. And something inside her crumpled, and she looked at Ford, whose face suddenly changed. She felt all the warmth inside leave her, leave her hollow, and she caved in and collapsed onto the floor.

"He trusted me, Ford. He thought so much of me, trusted my judgment."

Ford's shoes were tumbled over and empty in front of her, and his gray heather socks were next to her, still on his feet. He took a long deep breath, and she imagined him covering his face. He blew out in three forceful spurts, a singer's breathing exercise. Then his knees bent, and he was squatting next to her, his hand resting light on her head. She looked away from him, at his empty shoes.

In the silence, she heard a low buzz vibrating from her purse, underneath the pile of her clothes, an arm's length away. Her phone. Ford stood up, and she groped for her bra.

* * *

Nineteen-year-old Morgan sat down at the Steinway in Dad's music room. She looked again at her bandaged wrist, knowing it was too soon to start playing again but fearing even more that it was too late.

The bright winter sunlight streamed in through the big window at the back of the room. A bird feeder hung in the leafless redbud outside, but no birds were there. Morgan took a deep breath and started playing scales. She moved around and around the circle of fifths, first the major scales, then the harmonic minor, then the melodic minor. Finger memory was still with her after six weeks, and she missed only two notes. That was encouraging. There was a twinge of pain when she used the fifth finger of her left hand, but that was all.

Why did she have to cut that tendon? It was already her weakest finger.

She moved on to arpeggios—with her small hands it was even more important to keep up the arpeggios than scales. And her tendon hardly bothered her. In fact, it was fun! As she finished the arpeggios she was confident the "Butterfly" would fly, if not today, sometime before spring arrived. Her hands were warm, relaxed, and she dove in.

She expected the first few measures to be rough after not playing it for a few weeks. But every blasted huge five-finger chord sent a searing ring around her wrist. She kept playing. The pain spread to her hand and began to shoot up her arm by the 12th measure. She tried to pick up the tempo and soften the dynamics to take some of the pressure off, but it only got worse. She couldn't think, she couldn't interpret. She was running completely on finger memory and injured pride. You don't have the hands for Chopin! Leo Neville had sneered. And she didn't even like Chopin. Brooding, melancholy, diffuse—no precision of thought.

In the last score of the etude, she balled up her fists and slammed down on the keys. "I hate Chopin!" she blurted out.

"Then don't play him anymore."

Dad was standing at the door to the music room, trying to control his frightened expression. Morgan had tears in her eyes and looked away from him, back at the keys.

"I have to play Chopin. Everyone plays Chopin." Leo Neville couldn't be right. "Didn't you have to do exercises, go through the paces when you were a student?"

"Yeah. I had to jump through hoops." He put his hand on her shoulder. "But I managed to have some fun with the hoops." He stroked her hair for a moment, then stopped. "I'm almost done with this painting." He walked back to the door. "How about an invention? You always liked those. And somehow, Bach is just the right thing for finishing this off."

Morgan sniffed and wiped her nose with the back of her hand. "I haven't played any in a while. But OK."

"Play number eight. It's sunny."

"I'll give it a try. I'm sure I can play it better than you played 14."

Dad had already gone back to his studio, leaving the door open. Did she still know number eight by memory? Probably not. The book of inventions was sitting right in front of her, and she leafed through until she found the right page. Eight was a perky little number full of staccato and mock elegance. It reminded her of the more light-hearted of Mozart's pieces, but it was more precise, more spare, more elemental. And maybe more self-consciously laughing.

It did laugh, she thought as she began to play. She imagined two kids playing catch in Sunday clothes, daring each other to perform more and more complicated and risky gymnastic feats between catches. And every now and then, when the ball was in the air, the kids would cartwheel in unison and then laugh at the fact that they managed to pull it off.

When she finished number eight, her tendon was throbbing but not screaming. She started to play it again, and without thinking, she knew. She'd always go back to playing with the kids. It was where she belonged, not in Chopin's world of huge chords and amorphous moods. And that meant saying good-bye to Mount Hope, good-bye to the dream of concert halls and great acclaim. She broke into a quiet sob as she played the last measure, and her left wrist continued to throb in sympathy.

Morgan looked at her hands, knowing Leo Neville was right. And knowing that was enough to release all the desperation she had so carefully locked away. She got up from the piano and collapsed on the floor in a chorus of crying.

* * *

"Morgan? Thank God." Terence's voice had a military precision, as if the consonants were bullets. "Susan's water just broke. The poor woman will have to have the kid in County General—can't take a chance on heading out her way. I have to call you in—can you make it to the office?"

This speech had to make sense to Terence because he always made sense, but it made no sense to Morgan. Why wouldn't she be able to make it in? And Susan wasn't due for over a month.

"Yeah, I think I can make it in," she said, groggy. "What's going on?"

"Potentially significant ice. There's freezing drizzle right now over much of the central counties. But it looks like it'll get worse. We're starting to see convection over the front—in-cloud lightning even, and it looks like the overrunning's just getting stronger."

Ice, Morgan thought. In her mind, she could see the warm moist air running up over a wedge of cold air, heard the rumbling of thunder, felt the rain supercool as it fell.

"And where it's not raining, it's snowing," Terence went on. "Looks like we'll get at least six inches to the north and west. Where are you anyway?"

"Wolverton. But I haven't been near a window lately."

"Well, it's pretty gloomy. The front's stationary now, and it's not going anywhere soon. Jack is taking Susan to the hospital—"

"Is she OK?"

"She thinks so. Says it doesn't feel like anything's wrong, but it's so early, of course we're concerned. Jack will try to make it back to the office with some supplies in case we're here for a couple of days. Careful on the highway. The salt crews are out, but the front's sitting right on top of it. Keep your eyes out for lightning."

Morgan stood in the deserted corridor of the Civic Center near the entrance to the stairwell. Ford was still in the studio halfway down the hall. She hurried into the stairwell and started down just as Isabel reached the landing below.

Isabel paused as she turned up the last flight, her dark and perfect eyebrows arched knowingly. Morgan became aware of her own disheveled appearance, and she pulled her hand through her hair, back from her forehead.

"That was quick," Isabel said, showing her teeth in a derisive smile.

Morgan had nothing to say, though she took a deep breath in case anything came to her before she reached the landing.

Isabel caught her arm as she tried to move past. "I'd appreciate it if you didn't flaunt your infidelities to my daughter."

Beautiful Isabel looked as if she had scored a point, but Morgan wasn't sure what game she was playing. Isabel released Morgan's arm but held her gaze with deep brown eyes filled with vengeance. They narrowed, and then Isabel turned to resume her climb up the stairs. Morgan shook her head and let out a ragged breath.

Ford

Morgan just sank down and melted to the floor as if she were disappointed. Disappointed in what is the question. It was clear that it had nothing to do with me. It was almost insulting, her being so oblivious to me.

"He trusted me," she said. I thought at first she meant Rob trusted her to be faithful. But, as I said, it had nothing to do with me. She said, "trusted my judgment." She was talking about something else.

What could I do? She's a friend. That's the problem. She was sitting there crying, totally vulnerable, and I backed off. Because taking advantage of a friend is wrong. That must be it. But if I were such a good friend, I'd have asked her what she meant, let her tell me all about it. Helped her understand why she was so mad at Rob that she was there with me.

But that's not who I am. Just as well, duty called.

She left without even looking at me.

Then Isabel came storming in about five minutes later. Claimed she'd seen Morgan on her way up the stairs. She did seem to sense that our tryst had been something of a fiasco, as she launched into some kind of triumphant tirade. It was just steam, most of it. I looked at her pleasantly and said, "Is it about time for my aria? I think I'm going to head downstairs."

Isabel kept going. She just moved on to other people. When I got out onstage—the stage directions say, *Peter enters in a towering rage*, and it wasn't a stretch—I could see her out in the house, standing by the entrance, gossiping to every chorus member she could snag. It was easy to make Peter rail against the Borough gossips, and I'm afraid I was a little rough on the hapless apprentice too.

Then I saw Rob. Recognized him right away. He went up to Isabel—she was standing right by the lobby door—he probably asked if she'd seen Morgan.

Charles stopped me at that point. "Great emotion, Ford," he said. "But take it easy on poor Travis. He has to last through the whole run."

I apologized to the boy. "Keep the expression though," I said. "You look scared."

"And take it easy on your voice too," Charles went on. "It sounds great, but save it for the performances."

I nodded, but I was looking past Charles. The malicious delight on Isabel's face was unmistakable: she was telling Rob everything she knew as well as everything she presumed to know. She nodded her head in my direction. As the orchestra started up again, Rob looked at me as if he were going to march right up on stage and punch me in the face. But as I started to sing—*Go there!*—he seemed to make a decision. He left, Isabel still talking, still smiling in his wake.

I finished the scene about 10 minutes later, hitting my notes and my marks, playing it all very cool and restrained. I sang, *Now shut your eyes and down you go!* I sent the boy to his death, just as I'm supposed to, and then exited, hoping I wouldn't have to do it again.

Rob was waiting in the wings, clenching and unclenching his fists. I suddenly hoped Charles would call me back, demand more emotion this time.

Physical courage is not my forte. But bravado might be. I took a breath and said, "If you're going to hit me, just don't break my jaw. I have a show to do next week. I can still sing if I have a black eye, but a broken jaw would be incapacitating."

"Thanks for the suggestion," Rob said, applying more than enough sarcasm. "But I'm not inclined to indulge someone who's seduced my wife."

I tried to look surprised, but I doubt I pulled it off. "I've been trying to seduce your wife for years, and you've never hit me before."

"I wasn't actually planning on hitting you, but I'm reconsidering." He looked like it too, so I started moving away from him but sideways, like

I wanted to take the conversation elsewhere. He fell in, and we moved toward the dressing rooms, side by side.

"Look, Rob. I saw you talking to Isabel, and I have some idea what she told you. She's royally pissed off at me right now. You have no reason to believe anything she says. Or what I say. I might have reason to lie either way, and you don't know me well enough to tell whether I'm telling the truth. So what exactly do you want?"

Rob stopped and shook his head. I was relieved his hands were unclenched and stayed that way. "Where is she?" he said finally.

"Last I saw her, she took a phone call. I assumed it was you, but if it wasn't, maybe she was called in to work."

His angry expression melted into surprise. He looked almost happy—that struck me as odd. He turned to leave but stopped and looked back at me hard.

"Her phone rang. Was that before or after?"

"Before or after what?"

Rob didn't really want to know because he left after only a few more seconds of looking fierce.

My hands shook until I had to go back on stage. But I managed to text Morgan. I figured I should give her fair warning.

Nine

When Morgan came out of the Civic Center, a thin glaze of ice covered her windshield, very wet and easy to scrape away. The ice on the pavement was harder to deal with, however, and even harder to predict. There was a lot of traffic as usual in a college town on a Friday afternoon, and Morgan saw two fender-benders as she drove to the expressway interchange on the outskirts of Wolverton.

Once Morgan got on the highway, the weather seemed more promising. At first. Larger raindrops splattered against the windshield mixed with bits of slush—the water was partly freezing before it reached the surface. It was messy but not that dangerous. As she got closer to Richfield, however, the rain came down as pure liquid—supercooled and keen to freeze on contact wherever the surface temperature allowed. And more and more, the road surface was cold enough. She slowed down to watch for unsalted patches of pavement, while vehicles large and small sped past her, sometimes ending up in the ditch or on the median strip.

Just as she was passing a "Watch for ice on bridge" sign, a dark green pickup truck spun out of control on the overpass ahead. For a few slow-motion seconds, Morgan watched in horror as the pickup twirled 270 degrees, its rear banging against the concrete barrier to the side of the left lane, crunching the bumper and tailgate and snuffing out one of the brake lights. Morgan took her foot off the accelerator as her car climbed the gentle slope of the overpass. She kept her eyes on the road and crept by the pickup at 25 miles per hour.

A few miles outside Richfield, she was pretty sure she heard thunder, and the trees alongside the road looked like they'd had a long day. The power lines were still taut, but cold rain dripped too slowly from them, forming bumps of incipient icicles.

By the time Morgan arrived at the forecast office in Richfield, the ice had accumulated to almost an eighth of an inch on most surfaces. She slid into the parking lot, making as slow and wide a turn as possible. She wanted to park close to the entrance, but since that required making a sharp turn into a tight space, she opted for the row at the end of the lot that required no turning at all. The curb at the edge of the lot stopped her car when her brakes failed to, and she cut the engine and looked up at the Doppler radar tower that rose twenty yards directly ahead of her. She closed her eyes for a moment and felt the tension at the back of her head and behind her eyes melt enough to start hurting. She wished she could sublimate—go from solid to gas without this melting in between.

A loud insistent thudding next to her ear popped her eyes open and snapped her head back from the window.

"Morgan! You OK in there?" It was Jack. There was a deep crease between his eyebrows as he squinted into the car. He seemed to be much older than his 24 years, as if an extra decade of worry mapped his face. She wondered how old she was herself, how long she'd been asleep.

"Just dozed off, I guess," she yelled through the window. She unlocked the door, and Jack stepped back and put his hand on the hood for balance. She saw a small tear on the elbow of his jacket in the middle of a soaking wet spot. He'd taken a tumble on the ice all right, and she felt sorry for him, as if he were a little boy trying really hard at something and failing. She wanted to help him inside and make cocoa. Opening the door, she shook her head in the cold moist air, knowing she had to focus on something. Ice. It would be beneath her feet when she stepped out.

"Careful," Jack said. "I've slipped three times already."

"It wasn't nearly so bad in Wolverton."

"Probably wasn't the brightest idea calling you in, but with Susan going into labor—"

"How is she?"

"OK, far as I could tell. She's at the hospital now. She was a lot calmer than me, I can tell you! She was mostly worried her husband wouldn't be able to get there for the delivery."

Morgan shook her head again, hoping to clear it. She stood up with determination and held the car door as she tested the ice. "Slick." She stepped forward and turned around to face the door, and she and Jack gave it a gentle push to swing it shut. By instinct, neither wanted to make any sudden moves. A little momentum could carry you a long way today.

They crossed the ice in silence, negotiating their way around a slight slope into a drainage grate that Morgan had never noticed before. They both exhaled when they reached the sidewalk by the entrance, where a copious amount of melting compound had been spread. Several grocery bags sat in front of the door.

"You've been shopping," Morgan said, breaking into a smile.

"Yup. Terence's orders. Gotta feed the troops when they're in the trenches." They started to pick up the bags. They seemed very heavy. "You look real tired," Jack said.

"You just woke me up from a nap. Of course I look tired!"

Jack cracked a small smile. His laugh lines were deep and clear today, and his eyelids drooped a bit.

"You look tired too. And old."

Jack lost his smile in chagrined surprise.

Morgan laughed. "But not as old as I feel."

Terence met them as they carried the groceries into the break room. "Appreciate you coming in," he said to Morgan, and she believed him. As usual, his voice was sharp and quiet. "Wish you'd have gotten the sleep I ordered though." He poured coffee into her mug and handed it to her. His dark brown eyes looked a little watery, but that was the only sign of wear or strain on his face. He stood as straight as ever.

"I'm OK, sir," Morgan said and pulled herself up to her full height. "What do you want me to do?"

He thought for a moment, narrowing his eyes as if appraising her. He said, "Long-range forecasting. Have Wallace brief you and tell him to help Steve with the phones and texts so he can get on top of the nowcasting."

"I'm on it," Morgan said, almost spilling her coffee in her abrupt turn. She took two quick sips, as if that would restore the equilibrium in her cup, and the reduction in volume did in fact calm the waves.

Several phones were ringing in the front office and in the operations area. Reports, she knew, coming in from all over the region: snow, sleet, ice pellets, and rain, both the merely cold and the supercooled kind. Once she had gotten her briefing from Wallace, she pulled out her own phone. She didn't want to read Rob's texts or listen to his voicemail message, not right now, but she needed to tell him where she was. And he needed to stay put, not try to get home.

The most recent text wasn't from Rob though. It was from Ford: *Rob's looking for you.*

That was important?

That was important. Rob was at the Civic Center. Looking for her. Ford saw him. Did he talk to him?

Rob. She thought back to the expression that dawned on his face—like he'd discovered what the problem was and knew he'd find a solution. He was running after the solution now. He'd try to get home.

She dialed his cell number. He didn't pick up. She tapped her fingers against the desk while his voicemail greeting ran its course. "Rob? It's Friday afternoon, around five thirty. I got called in. Don't try to get back to Richfield—the ice is terrible. Wait out the storm." She felt like she should say more, but she didn't know what. "Please," she said at last, then hung up. She sent him a text: *I'm at work. Wherever you are, stay put! The ice is dangerous.*

She called their landline. No answer. She called his office phone. He didn't pick up. When she got his voicemail, she left another message. Then she hesitated for only a few seconds before checking her own voicemail.

There were now two messages. Rob's voice began, "Morgan? Where are you? We really need to talk. Call me, please?"

She heard him disconnect and the second message came on. It was Rob's voice again. "Morgan? Look, I'm at the Civic Center." In the long pause that followed, she could hear vague musical sounds in the background, and it sounded like Rob was moving. "I just talked to Isabel. I don't know what to think." His voice broke, a brief snag in the sound. "What the hell are you doing? I feel like I don't know you anymore!"

She felt betrayal searing her heart again, and this time it hurt. What the hell *was* she doing?

After another long pause, she heard his voice again, this time drenched with disgust: "Ford for Christ's sake!"

The message ended there in an electronic pulse.

She looked at Ford's text again. It came in after Rob's voicemail. Did Rob actually talk to Ford after he called? Did it matter?

She took a deep breath and blew it out. Then she put her phone away and turned to the computer screens. There was more than enough work to bury her worry, guilt, and shame. For now.

*   *   *

Eight hours later, the data flitting across Morgan's computer screens were discouraging, no matter how she viewed them. The storm system wasn't going anywhere for another six hours at least, and the northern boundary of the warm sector was likewise stationary. They could only hope that the warm layer would decay and the cold layer warm up through diabatic processes, but the convection along the front had intensified instead, and that strengthened the warm air overrunning and countered any cooling in the bright band. She began to think that maybe the answer lay in snow machines, which she imagined to be huge aerosol-spewing fountains, dancing to Handel's water music. Then she realized her eyes were closed. She opened them to jet stream data and another gulp of black coffee.

They had lost power a few hours before, their computer screens going blank in a pop of static, but their in-house generator was up and running in a matter of minutes. The landlines had gone dead around the same time, and not long after that, everyone's cell phones failed. Terence figured the ice must have broken something essential off the cell tower a quarter mile to their north. Their only communication with the outside world now came by police scanner, sporadic email, and data connections with weather service networks. They despaired of getting any news of Susan before the storm was over, and Morgan despaired of hearing from Rob.

She had become more worried as the evening drew on. She had tried calling Rob three times before they lost the phones, but he wasn't picking up, and she didn't know why. The last time she tried calling the landline, there had been no answering machine—the phone just rang and rang. No power apparently.

She was grateful she had work to do, something useful to focus on. When her turn came up to get a few hours of sleep on the hard couch in Terence's office, she tried to say no. But Terence insisted, and when he promised, with great tolerance, that yes, she could come back to work once she got some sleep, she lay down on the couch and remembered nothing else.

*　*　*

Although it couldn't have been more than a few minutes, it seemed to 19-year-old Morgan that an age had passed as she sat crumpled on the music room floor next to the Steinway. When at last she felt Dad's hand on her shoulder, however, she wouldn't look up at him.

"What's the matter?" he asked. "You played great." His arms were around her, and he kissed her hair. "Tell me what's wrong. Please."

"Leo Neville," she whispered, "doesn't deserve to be right."

"No, he doesn't." Dad knew the story, but he wasn't as angry as Morgan wanted him to be. "He doesn't matter," Dad went on in a soothing voice. "Don't let it matter, Morgan, what he thinks." He rocked her back and forth, and she smelled the paint on his clothes and the Fels-Naptha on his hands. "You be your own artist."

"I don't know how."

"Then you've got a lot to look forward to, learning." He lifted himself off the floor and offered her a hand. "Come on," he said. "I want to show you something."

She took his hand after a moment's hesitation. "The painting?"

Dad nodded as he pulled her up. "It's done. I think it's pretty good."

Morgan followed him down the three steps to the studio, curiosity piqued in spite of herself. She swiped her left hand under her eyes, using the gauze from her bandaged wrist to soak up the tears. The translucent blinds along the south wall were drawn against the bright sun. The painful black and red painting that he'd done when she was in the hospital was in the darkest corner of the room. Morgan turned away from it as soon as a quick glance told her it was there.

The new painting was set up on one of his big easels. About four feet by three feet, its background was a deep olive with yellower shading for texture. Two smooth black lines cut meandering paths from the upper right down to the lower left. Between them, the yellow shadings organized themselves into the foreground in a bright sunny stream. There were speckles of white, gray, and, above all, chartreuse. They floated near the surface of the painting, over the black lines and olive background, forming a clockwise swirl of bright green headed from center toward the lower right.

Morgan looked at Dad and giggled. "An Australian low pressure system?" she asked.

Dad laughed. "It's called *Weather Map*."

"No kidding." Morgan turned away from it to face Dad. "It's great, Dad," she said as she hugged him. "I really like it."

"Good. It's yours."

"Oh, Dad, no." She looked at him to see if he was serious. "You can sell this one. It's too good to give away."

"I don't feel like I'm giving it away. It's yours." He hugged her again and kissed her cheek. "I'll sell that other one." He motioned with his head toward the dark corner.

Morgan looked as she hung on to him and saw the red petals bleeding into the blackness. "Yes. Sell that one. It's good too."

"It is, isn't it? And I know someone else would appreciate it more than I do."

"Thanks, Dad." She let go of the hug. "I hope I can find a dorm room with enough wall space for it."

Dad's laugh was half-hearted, and Morgan noticed his tears for the first time. "The Mount Hope dorms are pretty small," he said.

"Probably like everywhere." She looked again at the bleeding petals and then back at Dad. "But I don't think I'm going back there."

"Please don't." He looked at her as if searching for confirmation that it didn't hurt as much as he feared. "It didn't seem good for you."

"I don't think it was." Pain burned hot in her wrist now, and she felt a sob forming in her throat. But she rallied and managed a smile. "Maybe I'll study meteorology in Australia."

"Or New Zealand," Dad said, playing along. "I always wanted to visit the Maoris."

Morgan stepped back, feeling awkward, and moved toward the door. "I guess you never know where life will take you."

"No," he agreed. "You never do."

She felt herself crying again, and she didn't like it.

"Morgan," he said, as if not knowing what else to say. "Nothing's ever final. As long as—you live."

She ran back up the three steps out of his studio and into the music room. A cardinal sat on the bird feeder outside the window amid the brilliant white of winter, pecking around for the few seeds that were left. "Well, we're alive," she said to the bird, and it flew away.

*   *   *

"Morgan?" A tentative hand pushed into her shoulder. "Time's up, Morgan. Time to get up."

Morgan opened her eyes and squinted at the gray light streaming in the window across the room. Terence's office. A hard couch. Jack's brown flannel shirt. He was squatting next to the couch, a two-day-old beard on his face and creased bags under his eyes. She rubbed what seemed like five minutes of sleep from her own eyes, though she figured it was probably six hours. "What time is it?" her voice cracked.

"Nine thirty." She heard the impatience in his voice, and there was longing for sleep in the creases of his frown. His expression softened as she sat up. "Sunday, in case you lost track."

She hadn't. She stood up, and Jack sat down. She'd been there almost 40 hours now, and Jack probably over 48. His torso flopped down, and his head hit the cushion where her head had rested seconds earlier. She bent down and lifted his feet to the couch. He looked surprised, but he closed his eyes before he said anything. It was a muttered syllable that could have been "Thanks."

She went over to the window, wagging her head from side to side, pulling her shoulders back in a compact stretch she had perfected over a long career as an accompanist. The rain had stopped. It had been just drizzle in the wee hours when she went to sleep, so it had probably been dry for three hours or so. Dry. The ice had hardened from its almost liquid state. It looked cold out. The storm system had moved east and dragged the warm sector along with it, and the wind was brisk from the east northeast. A few snowflakes were in the air, but the clouds would be thinning and high pressure would build in over the next 12 hours. The sun would heat up some dark surfaces, but it would be very cold again tonight. Most of this ice wasn't going to start melting for at least 24 hours.

The ice—three inches of it—coated everything in sight: the cars in the parking lot, the roads, the sidewalk. The trees across the road—bowed and broken, branches straining toward the ground. A few bare trunks stood upright but not proud. They swayed in the wind, and large chunks of ice popped off at strange angles dictated by some unholy collaboration of torque and gravity. It would all be a beautiful world of fairy glass by tomorrow, sunlight refracting through millions of ice prisms. Beautiful and deadly. Power and telephone lines were splayed across the road, their wooden poles having crashed to the ground long before.

"Morgan?" Terence whispered from the door to his office, calling her back from the window. "Let's get going. We still have freezing rain coming down from Conn County east."

Morgan nodded and pulled herself away from the icy picture outside.

Terence smiled as she came through the door. "Heard from Susan. Baby girl—four pounds, eight ounces."

"She all right? The baby—that's small, right?"

Terence shrugged. "It's a preemie. Incubator for a few days. Seems to be OK otherwise. I didn't get a lot of details. The phones are still down."

"How then—?"

"Email message from a nurse on the ward." He grinned and shook his head. "Susan. That's what I like about her. Where there's a will there's a way. Nice she thought of us."

Morgan smiled and started toward the operations area.

"Heard from Rob?"

"No." Even to her own ears, she sounded surprised. She stopped and looked back at Terence, not knowing why he'd asked or what he meant by the question.

"Sorry."

"We never caught up before we lost the phones." She looked down at the floor. "I'm pretty worried. I'm afraid he tried to come home from Wolverton and didn't make it."

Terence was silent for a moment. She didn't look at him. "Let's get back to work," he said as if offering a way out.

Rob

It felt like all the heat was leaching out of my body. I wanted to puke, but I didn't have the energy. I was covered with rain, soaked through, the ice under me melted.

That should've solved the problem, you'd think. I should've been numb. I was soaked through.

Waking up to pain isn't much of a relief, but the pain's there even when I'm asleep. Awake, at least the nightmares are less vivid.

If I drift off to sleep, I'll see his insufferable face, smiling. I really do want to smash his jaw, ruin his precious gig next week. I take a swing at him, and my hand shatters like thin ice. The pain makes me scream. He's lying on the floor, a whimpering wolf with a bloody lip. Morgan has his head in her lap, and she looks up at me, so angry. I show her my missing hand, throbbing at the end of nothing. She bites the air where my pain is hanging. I can't see it, but I feel it, and I scream again.

I wake up with my wrist screaming—for a painkiller. Sometimes I get one. It's just that as the pain in my wrist recedes, my thoughts go wild again, run off, ravage the peace. I see Morgan with Ford. He's laughing, she's angry. And I want to slug that smug face again.

"I've been trying to seduce your wife for years"—yeah, I know it, you bastard. She said you never had a chance.

Ford! How could she? Did she?

Is not knowing worse than knowing for sure? Is wondering worse than having it all spelled out in graphic detail?

Damn him. Damn opera and music and everything I know so little about.

I should have seen it coming, but how could I? I thought it was all about Dad. I never thought she'd look to someone else.

I look for her, and I can't find her. I'm climbing the stairs in our house, I can see them. I want her to be in the studio, waiting for me at the harpsichord, that filmy nightgown, the moonlight on her shoulders. But there's no music. My chest fills with dread, I hear my heart beating, the blood rushing through my body, my ears, I can't hear anything for the roaring. That's why there's no music. That has to be it. But at the door, there's something black inside. Not just dark but darkness. There's nothing else it can be.

Damn it, it hurts. This roaring in my ears, my wrist. I think blood is spurting out of my wrist. Then I realize it's hers, under water. What if I've let her swim out so far by herself she can't find her way back? She hardly sleeps at all these days.

Just lie down, Rob. She can't leave any more than you can get home right now.

I wish I had some paint. Some canvas. I'd love to paint her face from memory. In parts, an extreme close-up of her lips, her teeth. The curve of her neck, the play of shadows over her jugular. I could see it pulse sometimes if her neck was stretched out at just the right angle, blue moonlight glowing on the white sheet where she rests, the pulse in silhouette. I'd paint it like a snowbank—or something warmer, a sand drift, a dune that breathes, moves, twitches as the wind eddies around it.

Nothing's ever final. We just need more paint.

Ten

No one was home. It was obvious at a glance that no one had been home since the beginning of the ice storm. Rob would have spread a melting compound on the driveway and the front walk, would have cleared the front steps of ice.

The blank wall in the foyer seemed indifferent. Asleep. The whole house seemed asleep—dead even. Cold and stiff. It was almost freezing, literally, though not quite. Morgan blew into the air and nodded when she observed no vapor. She tried the kitchen light, but as she expected, it didn't come on. No power to the furnace, no power to the kitchen. A leftover mug of coffee stood on the kitchen counter thickening from evaporation.

If Rob had come home, he would have set the mug in the sink, maybe washed it. He would have turned on the generator.

She opened the basement door and flipped the light switch by force of habit. Then she made her way down the dark stairs, guided by the afternoon light from the small window over Rob's desk. As she stepped past his work area, she felt an unpleasant flutter in her chest that felt like regret.

She found the main water valve and turned it off in case the pipes had burst. Then she went to the generator's transfer switch, located in a dark corner next to the water heater. She felt the cold surface of the enclosure and opened it. When she turned the switch on, the generator in its shed outside buzzed to life, and she heard its faint throbbing through the earth for a few seconds before it settled back into a quieter rhythm, inaudible from the basement. The furnace and water heater both coughed, then hummed low with more vibration than tone. Morgan felt the side of the furnace down low and found it warm, pilot light still lit. She saw in the half-light that her hand was shaking, and she sank to the bare cement floor and cried.

Where was Rob? Was he hurt somewhere? Was he dead? Morgan shivered. At least seven people in the area had died in the storm. Traffic accidents mostly, and one man died out in Clayton County, electrocuted by a downed power line—that would never happen to Rob, but he might slip and fall, be hurt somewhere, somewhere cold, somewhere people wouldn't see or hear him until the storm was over and they ventured out of their homes again.

Stop it, Morgan, she told herself.

Why wasn't he home?

"Stop it!" she said and then got to her feet.

"Rob is fine," she said as she climbed the stairs. He knew enough to stay put in an ice storm. He was at the university somewhere, waiting with other people stranded by the storm, unable to call because the landlines were down and the cell towers damaged. But why hadn't he called before that?

"Stop it!" she said again. She was standing at the kitchen window, looking out at the shiny crust of ice on the backyard's refrozen snow. It was smooth and metallic. In her mind, she saw Rob on a stainless steel operating table, sitting on its edge in a white hospital robe, shaking his head, and smiling when he saw her. He lifted his hand toward her and almost fell over. Someone laughed. It might have been her.

"Don't laugh at me," he said, and his pout was so piteous that she had to fight to stifle a giggle.

"Of course not. I wouldn't do that."

She and the nurse helped him off the table to a stool behind a screen. She helped him get dressed. He was getting less groggy by degrees and more cranky. She responded to his grumpiness with long hugs and brief kisses. "Thank you for doing this," she whispered in his ear. "You're wonderful."

"This was a good idea, right?" he asked. He wouldn't have asked if he hadn't been weakened by the anesthetic. He knew he shouldn't have needed to ask.

It was her idea. Not the vasectomy itself but the reason for it. The vasectomy was his sacrifice to her good judgment.

The sun was bright. She could hear the ice melting—drips in the eavestrough, tiny pops on the roof as gravity pulled the ice apart. She heard the hum of the furnace far away, far below. She wasn't looking at the ice anymore. Her hands covered her face, trying to stanch the tears, the realization. Her scars throbbed, her left wrist, her right hand.

She was the reason they didn't have a family—she had always known that deep down, though they both said it was a shared decision. But why they *couldn't* have a family—that had been Rob's idea. And he'd had to ask her whether it was a good one.

He trusted her judgment.

She looked up at the empty and treacherous backyard, and a sheet of ice came crashing down from the roof. It seemed to have come from over her studio.

She snatched up her purse from the kitchen counter and strode through the house and up the stairs. The picture of Mom and the snow sculpture had rested in her purse for almost four days, and she took it out when she reached the studio and looked at it, memorizing her mother's smile. She set the picture on the harpsichord, her Kirckman replica, and turned around to face the closet.

Weather Map was in there. She had taken good care of it, and she knew its colors were as vibrant as the day 17 years ago when she realized she would never be a concert pianist. Her life had been good since then, a life with few regrets, a life full of music, weather, love. And family. She pulled *Weather Map* out of the closet and set it against the wall, out of the direct sun. For a long interval, she knelt in front of it, admiring the depth and texture of the greens and yellows, the fluid movement of the meandering black lines, the whimsical groupings of white, gray, and chartreuse. It was unlike anything else he had ever painted and still very much his own work. It made her feel like Dad was smiling at her. Like he was proud of her, proud to be her father.

Eventually, she sat down at the Kirckman replica and admired the painting from a different perspective. Her hands rested on the keys, and a few bars of Bach's three-part invention number eleven sprang to her fingers, the piece that accompanied Dad's mourning after Mom died. She stopped after four measures, however, not because of painful memories but painful sounds. Every note howled.

Of course it howled! Her instrument had been neglected in the coldest, darkest months of the year. She reached behind her and held a hand over the heating vent beneath the window. The rising air was warm. Good. She stood up, took off her coat, then pulled her tuning fork and tuning hammer out of the harpsichord bench.

If she had wanted to play, she would have sat down at the upright across the room or gone downstairs to the Steinway—by instinct, she would have chosen an instrument that held its pitch better through heat, cold, humidity, time. But she had sat down at the harpsichord, knowing it would hurt to hear the product of her neglect. It was time to appease the wolves. To make amends. It was not a perfect world, but some things could be coaxed into order and beauty, even with a great flaw in their midst. The flaw itself was a miracle of imperfection.

She struck the tuning fork, sounded an A, and listened.

* * *

The sun was low in the sky, and dusk was ready to pounce. Morgan was finishing up tuning the back eight-foot choir, matching each string unison for unison with the already tuned front. The house was otherwise still, and Morgan tried to concentrate on the sound, listening for beats. She listened for beats in unison tones and for the sound of Rob's car in the driveway.

She was almost ready to move on to the four-foot choir when she heard someone step onto the front porch. There had been no car driving up, no door slam. She held her breath for the doorbell, fearing bad news. When the key rasped in the lock, she ran down the stairs and stopped on the landing when she saw Rob step into the living room.

"Rob? What happened? What happened to your arm?"

His right arm was in a sling. He needed a shave, and she was startled by how much gray was in his whiskers. He looked so much older. But he smiled as he came up the short flight of stairs to the landing. He hugged her with his left arm, and she pressed her forehead into his prickly cheek. He smelled faintly like antiseptic, and she put her arms around him, grateful to have him back.

"I got in a fender bender when I got off the highway to Richfield—"

"You shouldn't have tried—I called you, told you to stay in Wolverton."

"I got out because I didn't want to get hit by some other idiot trying to drive in the storm, but that was pretty stupid. I slipped and broke my fall with my arm. Cracked my wrist."

"Oh, God, that must have hurt."

"I think I went into shock. The police were there—the accident, it had a lot of cars to it, it seemed like—and they got me to the hospital. By the time they took care of my wrist, there was no question of trying to leave." He hugged her tighter. "I wish I could've called. The phones have been down for a long time."

"They're down everywhere—"

"So I just walked home. Seemed safer than driving—"

"Walking's how you got hurt!"

"And I have no idea where the car is!"

"We got our landlines back at the office this morning. I kept trying to call you."

"My phone still has no service."

"Neither does mine. I keep picking it up expecting to be able to text you."

He hugged her for a long moment without either saying anything, and then he loosened his grip and stepped away. He looked at her and worked his jaw for a moment. "You did get my messages though? Before the phones stopped working?"

She looked down. Her arms fell to her sides. Her heart raced, and her skin felt clammy. She took a deep breath and looked up. His face was calm and serious. She felt as if she had deepened the lines in it, marked him indelibly.

"I'm sorry," she whispered. "I wish it hadn't happened." She looked down again. "I mean, it … it didn't. But it might have. I … let too much happen."

Rob cupped his left hand behind her neck, and she tilted her head up. "We can't let these things happen," he said in his softest voice. Then he kissed her hard.

She nodded even while she kissed him. When he looked at her again, she knew he was hurt, even though he looked relieved. "It won't happen again," she promised.

He looked away a moment and shook his head. "There's no excuse. Of course. But there have to be reasons. I don't know if I want to know what they are." He looked back at her. "But I probably should." He nodded at her. "Right?"

"I don't think I know all the reasons. But I want to show you something." She drew him up the stairs.

"You've been tuning!" he exclaimed. Morgan hated the look of joy on his face.

"Yes," she said, letting go of his hand. "I've been terrible lately—and not just to you. It was so out of tune. It hurt to hear it." She was crying, damn it. "Don't look so happy, Rob. Please. It hurt to hear it."

Rob's mouth stopped smiling, but his eyes were still happy. That was OK, she found. That was OK. He put his arm around her. "I'm sorry."

"No," she snapped, but she drew him to her fiercely. "*I'm* sorry. It's my fault. I stopped taking care of so many things—important things. I'm so sorry for that. I'm sorry I slapped you—I'm sorry I was so angry and I didn't stop to figure out why. I'm sorry for everything."

He nodded as he held her, and she felt some relief, a lifting of some of the shame she had not wanted to look at.

After a moment, he said, "Was it *Weather Map* you wanted to show me? It's nice to see it again, anyway."

"It is nice to see it again. It's not what I wanted to show you though." She pulled away and picked up the photograph of the snow sculpture.

"Your mom, right? That's a great sculpture. It's quiet but powerful too. And that's you? Next to the sculpture?"

"Incidental."

"Incidental?"

"I was incidental."

"You do look unhappy."

"And Mom's really happy. The happiest I remember her. She sculpted that snow, knew exactly what she was doing."

"I knew she was a sculptor. I've never seen any of her work though."

"She gave it up. Her works were too big, needed too much space, were too expensive to cast." She shook her head hard. "But she knew what she was doing. I was building a snowman too that day. I worked hard at making the big snowballs just perfect, and she took them apart, hacked them up with a saw. Made it a part of her sculpture." She was crying hard now. "She didn't even notice how it made me cry. And still, I admire her for it." She wiped away some of her tears and looked at Rob. He was listening hard, and he wasn't smiling at all. "That scares me, Rob."

"She probably thought she was involving you in something she loved." Rob looked back at the photograph. At her.

"You think so?"

He nodded. "It's what I would do." He looked at her with a slight smile. "What would you have done?"

"If I were a sculptor?" She shrugged. "Probably something of the same thing. I hope I would've noticed if my daughter was upset though. But … "

"What?"

"But she had left sculpture behind. Gave it up. Getting a taste of it blinded her."

He looked at her, puzzled. "Maybe if she hadn't given it up altogether, she wouldn't have been so blinded? Smaller works, fewer than she wanted, but enough to keep her hand in?"

A sob rose in Morgan's throat. She choked out, "I'm so sorry, Rob. You should've had kids. I'm so sorry."

"Morgan," he said, touching her face. "That was *our* decision."

She shook her head. "It was what I wanted, and"—a flash of that outpatient operating room distracted her—"and I think I've been blaming you for making it final. And I think you've been blaming me—"

"Morgan—"

"Or maybe I'm just blaming myself. But it was me—the whole reason—"

"Hey! That's not the way to look at it."

"So I'm sorry."

He took her face in his hands and made her look him in the eye. "You were all the family I was sure I wanted—I don't regret the decisions we've made. You were most important."

"That's the problem—if I was most important, I was responsible. And I do regret it. It hurt you. And it hurt me."

"If I'd insisted on having children, would you have left me?" She looked away, and he dropped his hands. She looked at the photograph.

"I was scared I would. I was scared I wouldn't. I don't know what I would've done."

"I don't know what you would've done either. But don't you think I would've found out, would've pushed harder, if I hadn't had misgivings about kids myself?"

Yeah, she thought. Rob was thorough when he looked things over.

"And you know, Morgan, it doesn't have to be final."

She looked back up at him. His eyes looked hopeful, and his mouth twitched like he was suppressing a smile.

"We could adopt?"

"Sure. Why not? If that's what we wanted." He shrugged. "I could even get another operation, if we wanted to try to have our own."

She put her arms around him and held him tight, her head against his chest. She heard his heart quicken, and she felt short of breath. "I'm scared to death, Rob. I'm scared to disappoint you again. Scared not to."

"I'm scared too." He pushed her hair back from her forehead, his fingers lingering at the back of her head, combing the loose tangles. "It's not like we made a bad decision." He drew her head back and kissed her. Then he looked into her eyes and smiled. "But we need to decide again. That's not such a bad thing."

"Nothing's ever final, I guess."

He grinned. "Like Dad used to say."

"He said that?"

The doorbell rang. They looked at each other with a question mark between them, and both shrugged at the same time.

As they went down the stairs, Morgan squeezed Rob's hand and said, "Thanks for coming back."

"You're welcome."

She stopped and looked up at him. He was smiling, but it wasn't a joke.

"Good to know," she said, serious, then squeezed his hand again.

They opened the door to Tracy and Stu, each holding a small crying child bundled up against the cold. The adults both looked ragged, faces splotchy with cold and strain.

Stu said, "Sorry to bother you, but we saw smoke coming out your chimney. We haven't had power for three days, and we're freezing. Would you mind if we came inside for a while and warmed up?"

"Of course not!" both Morgan and Rob said, already pulling them inside.

"I'm sorry I didn't think of you earlier," Morgan said. "I turned the generator on a couple of hours ago when I got home from the forecast office. It's been a long, long weekend. Here, let's get the little ones out of their coats and let them run around a bit."

"Thanks," Stu said, looking sheepish but relieved. "Power's out all over the neighborhood."

"All over the county," Morgan said. "And parts of 24 other counties and two other states. It's been a nasty storm."

Rob was helping Tracy take off the kids' jackets and hats. Tracy was scrupulous in avoiding eye contact.

Stu said, "What happened to your arm, Rob? Are you OK?"

"Slipped on the ice, broke my wrist."

Stu winced in sympathy.

"The doctor said it should heal fine. Why don't I get a fire going?" He looked at Tracy. "The kids would probably like that?"

Tracy smiled a little and said in a small voice, "Yeah. That'd be great."

"The water's turned off until we can check the pipes, but I think there's enough in the refrigerator to make some coffee," Morgan said, "and I'll scare up some hot chocolate, too."

"Need any help?" Stu asked.

"No, why don't you help Rob with the fire? He could use another hand."

"Ha ha," he said and went into the living room, where Tracy and Rob had herded Katie and Mac.

Rob joined her in the kitchen just as she put a pan of milk over a low flame on the stove.

"Should we invite them to stay the night?" he asked.

"Of course."

"I just hope it doesn't last a week."

"Take it as it comes," she said. "Might be a good opportunity to see what life with a family is like."

"Life with kids," Rob said, sounding like he was correcting her.

She looked at him, questioning.

"We don't need to have kids to be a family."

She drew his left hand up to her lips and nodded. The world was melting, she thought. It felt like spring.

"Thank you," she said and smiled against his hand.

Postlude

It was an extravagance to give a harpsichord an entirely new temperament to play one four-minute piece. But wasn't it an extravagance to even own a harpsichord in the 21st century? For that matter, wasn't buying a painting, studying opera, composing a symphony that no orchestra was ever likely to play, an extravagance? Any single artistic gesture, whether of creation or consumption, looked like an extravagance from a practical perspective. Yet Morgan knew that music was essential to her life, and painting was now essential to Rob's—art provided them both with a lifeline of joy. Perhaps it was more valuable because it didn't provide them a living as it had for Dad. So Morgan had embraced the extravagant gesture and tuned her Kirckman replica to play William Albright's "Danza ostinata" for Rob.

Morgan pulled a heavy deep-pile carpet remnant out of her studio's closet, which she brought out only for certain special occasions. It was a dull color, but it had a padded backing and was exceptionally soft. As she unrolled the carpet on the open floor space between the harpsichord and the upright piano, she thought with satisfaction of the extravagant care she had given to arriving at just the right temperament for the Albright.

The choices were legion, and she hadn't wanted to be altogether arbitrary in her starting point. Albright didn't appear to compose with a particular temperament in mind, but she did know that "Danza ostinata" had debuted on a replica of a classic French harpsichord. Moreover, Albright had numbered Messiaen among his strongest influences. So she decided to start with a French temperament, Rameau's *tempérament ordinaire*, and make adjustments from there.

Her primary concern for this piece—for any piece she played for Rob—was for the purity of the intervals of the final chord. She had taken her time experimenting with it, widening then narrowing the major fifth until she'd found the sound she wanted, the one that was the most powerful, that rang the loudest and the longest. The final chord was supposed to last three quick beats, not much longer than a second, but when she was playing for Rob, she never released the keys until the sound ran out of its own accord. Albright would just have to forgive her final fermata.

She shook out a soft flannel sheet and spread it over the carpet. As she smoothed it out to the remnant's edges, she smiled in anticipation of her brief recital, the final chord, and the postlude that would play out afterward on the floor.

The Albright had been a challenge to learn. "Danza ostinata" was the final movement of a suite called *Four Fancies*, which she had admired as a student but never actually liked. Until now, she had never tried to play any of the four, least of all the last. It had intimidated her. She hadn't believed she possessed the skill to master its massive tone clusters, tricky rhythms, and time signature changes at performance tempo. However, it was a piece that she was sure Rob would like.

It was all about forward motion, patterns and breaks of pattern. It had a compulsive racing rhythm that would remind him of Khachaturian's "Sabre Dance," one of his favorites in the orchestral repertoire. The mechanical ostinato in the bass made her picture a street sweeper, and that alone was temptation enough to learn it for Rob. And the more she listened to it, the more she saw what Rob would see: vertical loads compressing surfaces, shear forces pummeling bridges, the interplay of centripetal and centrifugal forces as tires hugged the curves of a road, and near the end, explosions of color in brutal downbursts of sound.

It was a piece that had to be memorized. At performance tempo, it was impossible to read the score, much less turn pages. Everything about it—notes, fingerings, articulations, register changes, time signatures, and, above all, rhythms—had to be ingrained, not only in muscle memory but deep in her psyche. In performing this piece, there was no time even for thought—thinking, in fact, would be disaster. Everything had to be instinctive.

But while she was learning "Danza ostinata," there was plenty of time for thought, plenty of time to contemplate the intricacies of the piece that no one, even Morgan herself, would hear at tempo. She had time to feel the weather in it, the terrible power of the jet stream, the building of a storm cell's towering cumulonimbus, the sublime terror of a massive shelf cloud moving over the prairie.

As she increased the tempo in rehearsal, the sky disappeared, and the work became more earthbound. Hail pelted pavement, the air popped with the punch of a jackhammer, and gravel began to fly. She knew she was approaching mastery when she found herself behind the wheel of a sports car, racing around tight S-curves way over the speed limit, challenging the angle of the banking to the point the tires were about to leave the road surface.

Now, after weeks of practice, the piece was ready for Rob. And she was ready to play it.

She stood up from smoothing out the flannel sheet and looked around the studio. The floor was clear of random scores and other small hazards, the closet was closed, and the window curtains were open to let in the moonlight.

She sat down to warm up. With both hands on the lower manual, she played four octaves up and down a C Mixolydian scale. She figured that was the key of "Danza ostinata," though she wasn't in fact certain. She laughed at how concerned she used to be about such a minor point. The key was hardly relevant in a piece like this, even to trained ears. She moved her hands to the upper manual and played the scale again. And then again with her right hand on the upper manual and left hand on the lower. She went through the same routine with a C-major arpeggio, then rose from the bench.

The harpsichord sounded marvelous. Her hands felt strong and powerful.

She turned out the lights and opened the door of the studio. She gave her eyes a few moments to adjust to the darkness. It was a clear night outside. The world was tilting toward summer. It was between 12:30 and 1 a.m., and the bright gibbous moon had just slipped over the neighborhood's rooftops. As she knew it would, the moonlight bathed the room in cool bluish light. The temperature, however, was warm, warm enough for her hands, warm enough for her bare shoulders.

She opened the lid of the harpsichord's case, then sat down again. She sounded the final chord of the Albright and let it ring out to the last vibration, a kind of clarion call to Rob. He was asleep downstairs in their bedroom, but he would soon wake up. He always woke up when she played for him.

She took a deep breath and relinquished control to her well-trained hands. They launched into the ostinato's sudden riveting. After four quick measures, a fast car careened past the street sweeper, and the four-minute race to the end was on. Morgan took blind curves with closed eyes, plunged down steep inclines without brakes, flew over deep chasms without wings. Pitches piled up in her right hand, receded, then piled up again in waves—four-, five-, even six-note clusters, and her Kirckman replica became as loud as a harpsichord could get, enveloping her in a thick batten of sound waves that absorbed any mistakes she made.

Her fingers crashed to a sudden landing on the final C-seven chord—luminous thirds with the wild beating of the minor seventh against the tonic. Her mind found focus again in that motionless moment. It didn't matter whether Albright forgave her that final fermata. This was for Rob, and he was standing in the doorway. As she held the keys, she allowed the corner of her mouth to smile and with a slight turn of her head slipped him a look out of the corner of her eye. He knew exactly what she was doing, and when her eyes met his, his lips had no time to smile.

Acknowledgments

Gratitude and admiration to:

Dan Hoyt and his students in literary editing at Kansas State University, whose creativity and judgment made *Unequal Temperament* a better book.

Jean Barrett and Joan Kessler, creative women who responded with great insight to an early draft. I am also grateful for their sustained and sustaining friendship over many years.

Ray Wolf, the science and operations officer at the National Weather Service's office in Davenport, Iowa, who generously shared his expertise and experience with me.

The Djerassi Resident Artists Program, which gave me not only the gift of time to work on this book but also the company of visual and musical artists whose influence haunts these pages.

Tom De Haven, who told me I was going to make it as a writer at a time I really needed to hear it.

Bruce Hart, whose creativity, moral support, and good humor are peerless. I love you madly.

www.ingramcontent.com/pod-product-compliance
Lightning Source LLC
Chambersburg PA
CBHW050343160726
48002CB00001B/436